The author was a young barrister when he got the case of the real Isabel Earl who was tried at the Old Bailey charged with capital murder.

He remained a practising barrister doing first criminal and later commercial cases, subsequently becoming a Recorder of the Crown Court and Deputy Coroner to the Royal Household.

He then accepted an offer from Lloyds Bank to become its Chief Legal Advisor. As an expert on Banking Law, Derek Wheatley has written many articles for newspapers and the legal journals; this however is his first novel.

The Silent Lady

Derek Wheatley

The Silent Lady
(Mona Lisa)

Vanguard Press

A CIP catalogue record for this title is
available from the British Library.

ISBN 978 184386 425 7

Vanguard Press is an imprint of
Pegasus Elliot MacKenzie Publishers Ltd.
www.pegasuspublishers.com

First Published in 2008

Vanguard Press
Sheraton House Castle Park
Cambridge England

Printed & Bound in Great Britain

Acknowledgement

"I am very grateful to Nigel Eastman,
Professor of Law and Psychiatry, London University, who
was the greatest help to me on the subject of
hysterical aphonia and related mental defences."

"Where shall I begin, please your Majesty?" he asked.
"Begin at the beginning" the King said, gravely, "and go on till you come to the end: then stop".

Alice in Wonderland
Lewis Carroll

Chapter One

For most of us the choice of a career is a difficult one. But not for me. I was going to become a barrister; I had decided this at an early age. Reading the "Life of Edward Marshal Hall", the celebrated Edwardian Defender, seeing "The Winslow Boy" at the theatre and visiting the Courts in the Castle at Exeter, had left me with a glamorous, not wholly realistic idea of my future career, but I knew that it was what I had to do, and nothing else. I wanted to defend the innocent, make pleas for leniency for the guilty, pursue the ideal of justice for all my clients. I was young enough to be an idealist; not practical enough to see, let alone be deterred by, the several pit-falls there might be in a career which was best suited for the well to do, which I was not. Much better for those with a strong legal connection, so that a solicitor uncle or two could provide the early briefs, whereas I had no uncles at all but only aunts; and they were certainly not in legal practice of any kind. But my own determination remained. Perhaps I might be the first Pearse to become a barrister, but I SHOULD be the first… and perhaps not the last either. I would have to get some clients; and I would first have to become qualified to do so.

But I was only a boy in my teens still at school; first of all there was the tiresome business that there was a war going on. In Exeter this meant that there were air raids to be endured. The Germans had decided on the tactics of bombing our most beautiful cities; Salisbury, Bath, Coventry and Exeter were all targeted. A famous German pre-war Guide, had gone into raptures about these beautiful English cities. The enthusiasm of the authors had indirectly caused the wartime raids upon them which caused such devastation, the destruction of Coventry Cathedral amongst it. It had been intended to wipe them out altogether, becoming infamous as the Baedeker raids. The idea had been to hit the British where it hurt and, of course it had. But the Churchill spirit was very much with us; so that the desired effect, to so shatter us that we should immediately sue for peace at any price, resulted only in steelier determination by the British and a greater hatred of the Hun however much we hated to see the devastation caused to our loveliest cities none of which could ever have been described as a military target. I remember cowering under the stairs at night in the middle of a raid with my parents. We had been woken up from sleep by the eerie wailing of the sirens, with no time to get to the air raid shelter in the garden. For a boy of 14, brought up on stories of the adventures of the Famous Five in the Magnet and the Gem schoolboy weeklies, there was excitement mixed with real fear. Yes, just for a moment when a bomb went off much too close for comfort and the blast shook our family home to its foundations. But the next day the fear had gone and only the excitement remained. I remember that I had got out my bike and cycled round the smoking ruins taking photographs of the damage, only to be stopped by the police. Even a schoolboy with a brownie camera could not be allowed to do such a thing. The photographs might be of propaganda value to the enemy. The schoolboy might not be what he seemed. After they had asked some questions, and closely examined my identity card, my film was confiscated but after a solemn warning, I was at last allowed to cycle off home.

And so the years passed and at 18 I enlisted in the army. My wartime service meant first a six month course at a university. It did not matter that there was a fierce war going on or that London was now subject to attack by Doodle Bugs and the even deadlier V11 rockets. It did not matter that our forces were gathering on the South Coast, together with our allies and that D-Day Europe was about to come. Any young soldier who wanted to become an officer and passed a War Office Selection Board, might be chosen to go to University. There he would receive a special course of training to be worthier of the King's Commission it was expected he would attain. It all seems rather strange now, but that is the way it was, and I did want to become an officer. My elder brother John had just been awarded a Military Cross while fighting his way up Italy with a Reconnaissance Regiment equipped with Scout Cars, Armoured Cars and "half-tracks". The love of glamour, which had played some part in my decision to become a barrister, was already there, and I was determined to follow in his footsteps.

However by the time I had done all the basic training, and had learned how to drive several British and American tanks and how to fire their various guns, and how to map read, and how to operate the radios, and how to sit with my head out of the turret so that I could see to command them and had passed through my Officer Cadet Training Unit, the war was nearly over. By the time I had "passed out" as an officer and been commissioned it was quite over. But there was still a need for an army to occupy the conquered Germany so that I was sent out to join an armoured regiment in the British Army of the Rhine. I was no longer subject to all the dangers of war, but was just at the start of a new life as a very junior officer in a regiment which had been through the whole war. The 8th Hussars had been at El Alamein, had suffered under the fierce German attacks led by

Field-Marshal Rommel, then they had fought their way up Italy and finally returned to England to be part of the great allied assault across the English Channel on D-Day. So my new colleagues were experienced fighting men; but they never forgot that they had, some of them at least, been part of the regular peacetime Army.

They had been, and now they were once more, a regular Regiment of Cavalry. And the regiment had been one of the five which had formed the Light Brigade at Balaclava, that most famous of legendary acts of heroism which had always been doomed to disaster. But it had been glorious, so far as the regiments involved had been concerned, rather than the generals who ordered the charge, and would ever afterwards be remembered as the epitome of bravery. So, never mind that they had had little to do with horses over the past few years, by the time that I had joined them, the regiment had acquired some 75 horses. All were healthy and good looking, or they would not have been there. How they had been acquired I never found out. But for a Germany newly ravaged by the conquering allies, desperately short of food and every other important thing in life after six years of war, the opportunities for barter must have been many and easy. Be perhaps the reality was that when the war was still on, it was possible to requisition any necessary supplies and now the war was barely over, so who could object? There they were and now they formed an important part of the life of the regiment newly returned to peace and the duties of occupying Germany, until the politicians decided what was to be done with them. And of course, the horses were now an important part of life. Not only was there a daily early morning riding school for young officers, but there was every opportunity to ride out in the woods surrounding Lingen in North Germany where we were stationed.

My friend Johnny Dunn had been part of the reason that I had joined the 8th Hussars in the first place. The Regiment had a glamorous uniform with chain mail on the shoulders of the mess blues and a dark green "tent cap" with gold braid all over it, which was worn even with battle dress. This, coupled with their reputation as one of the five regiments which had charged at Balaclava, was quite enough to make them my choice, even though my own connections with Ireland were tenuous. It is true that there had been a Padraig Pearse who had taken part in the notorious Post Office Siege of 1916, which had led to the eventual separation of Eire from Great Britain. Although my own ancestors were solidly from Devon and Cornwall I knew that Padraig figured somewhere in the family tree as a remote cousin. But that was all; the rest of the Pearses seemed to have been rooted firmly in the West Country. But Johnny Dunn was certainly Irish and had had no hesitation at all; he was going to be an 8th Hussar. We had been good friends ever since we had both been Officer Cadets at Sandhurst and it would be good to keep that friendship up.

And Johnny was a much better horseman than I was, so that it was a pity that on one fine afternoon after work for the day had ended, and we decided to go out for a gentle ride in the forest, that the groom gave me Pluto, the Regiment's prize jumper to ride.

"She hasn't been out for a couple of days, Mr Pearse, so she needs the exercise badly," he said "...but maybe you'd better be a little bit careful of her... she might be just a little bit frisky."

Well I knew already that Pluto was a decidedly frisky lady and I decided to keep her on a short rein and be very careful indeed. So that it was sheer bad luck that, just as we approached the stretch of the forest where the real horsemen in the Regiment practised the gallop, my right stirrup leather suddenly broke. For the really experienced horseman this should have made little difference. The rider keeps his seat by the strong pressure exerted by his knees on the horse's back below the saddle. But I was not that experienced rider and it made a difference. At least it seemed to make a difference to Pluto. She saw the gallop ahead. She needed no urging to break into a frenzied gallop after her days of rest. But the pressure on her back was all wrong. So she decided to do something to put it right. She bucked and she reared. I managed to stay on her back, but I was gripping the reins much too hard and she bucked and she reared again and again. And eventually Pluto won... we parted company. I took off very fast and was only stopped when my head, protected only by a service cap, hit a tree.

The next thing I really remembered was sitting in the Mess with a cup of tea in my hands next to Johnny, and hearing Punch O'Mara, the Senior Major and in charge of all the horses, asking anxiously, "Johnny I hear you and Tam had an accident with Pluto..."

"Yes, Punch but it wasn't really Tam's fault at all..."

"No... never mind that now, these things happen... but how's the mare?" Punch asked anxiously, Pluto was after all the very best jumper the Regiment had and was entered for the Dortmund Horse Show in just a few days' time.

"The Mare's fine, Punch."

"Are you sure ...nothing damaged at all? Are you quite sure she'll be all right for the show on Saturday?"

"No, no she really is just fine."

"Well that is a relief." Punch sat back and visibly relaxed "...and how's Tam?"

It was important to get one's priorities right. A whole wartime of fighting had certainly taught Punch that at least. And Johnny had been very good. As I now found out, as my senses gradually came back to me under the influence of the warmth of the Mess, the friendly banter; "...so who came off his horse just on a quiet afternoon's hacking?" and the hot tea and buns that I was eating with undiminished appetite. Johnny explained that he had first galloped after Pluto and caught her, and brought her back for me, and then he had managed to get me onto the back of his own horse, so that he could lead me home very firmly and slowly riding Pluto without one stirrup. I had survived the mishap well. My head was hard. I was sent out riding again at once to steady my nerves. I even managed soon afterwards, to have a successful ride on Pluto herself who seemed to bear me no grudges as I bore none to her; after all it was "only her instinct and nothing personal at all" as the Farrier Sergeant had assured me.

Life with the British Army of the Rhine included other relaxations, which were strange for me and a change from the Britain at war that I had known. There were the frequent weekends in Holland. It was illegal at that time and a court martial offence, to "fraternise" with the Germans. Since we were occupying Germany this meant that the only available young women were the few girls who worked in the NAAFI, who were in very great demand, and "off-limits" for officers anyway. So that effectively there were no young women available which was very sad for young officers most anxious to fraternise with any pretty girl and to take her out for a drink, but luckily there was a remedy close to hand at the weekends. Lingen was quite near to the Dutch border and it was easy enough to get weekend leave and the use of a Jeep for a few of us to visit Enschede, the town close to the border, full of pretty Dutch girls.

The British had just liberated Holland after years of occupation by the Nazis. And the Dutch were very nice, friendly people who were very grateful and hospitable to their liberators.

We found that Enschede had already surprisingly returned to life, almost as we remembered that it had once been in England before the war. It was a great contrast to the very slow return to peacetime normality in England itself. At home there was still rationing and even more of the necessities of life such as bread, had actually become rationed, after the war officially ended on D-Day. It all seemed to be very strange but in Holland, which had been occupied for most of the war years, it was already possible to get very good meals in the restaurants and to find very good entertainment in its hotels and nightclubs. And it was all very cheap. A very good weekend in Holland cost almost nothing at all, in actual money. It could not. We were paid in pounds but in occupied Germany, there was only token paper money, known as BAFS, for use in the canteen, and there was no way of exchanging any BAFS for guilders, because they were not really currency at all but only token money. But the oldest way of all was there. It was possible to barter and the Dutch were very short of two things at least that made life worth living for so many; that is cigarettes and drinks. But the British Army had plenty of both. We had a free issue of 200 cigarettes a week and German Gin cost only three shillings a bottle. So the weekend Jeep to Holland would contain a small cargo. The Hotel Porter at the Hotel Der Graff would discretely collect this on arrival and just as discretely, and with great honesty, would hand over the proceeds of the barter. And we made some very good friends in Enschede and had some very good times. Feelings against their recent occupiers were naturally not very warm. I remembered that on one occasion, when in a party at the local nightclub, I sent a note to the leader of the group asking him to play the then very popular song "Hoch mien lieb, Violetta". He came to our table looking very uneasy because he had to refuse me; he explained that unfortunately he could not do this. "Hoch mien lieb" was a German song and if he played it everyone would get up and go out. "Wish me luck as you wave me Goodbye" after the ever popular Gracie Fields proved an easy compromise, but was still not quite the same.

Life in the 7th Armoured Division in Germany centred round Bielefeld and in particular round our own barracks, in Lingen, where the Colonel of the Regiment had already made some friends among the local Germans. It all seemed rather odd to me that the strict rule against fraternising with the local Fräuleins did not seem to extend to the local nobility; or in particular to our Commanding Officer who had met the local Margrave. Of course the Margrave had never been a Nazi, but was a great horseman, now without a decent horse. So it was no wonder that he showed a lot of interest in the regiment's horses. In exchange for the occasional loan of a mount, we were invited to shoot in his extensive forests. My own experiences as a hunter had previously been very limited and extended only to shooting rabbits and the odd hare, over the land of a friendly farmer in Devon. My philosophy about taking animal life was simple. I did not like the organised pheasant shoots I had been taken on. The line of beaters driving the pheasants to cross the line of fire of the waiting guns, was too much like a slaughter for my own tastes. It is true that the guns were allowed to take home a brace of pheasants for the pot, so that I could pretend to myself that it was quite all right because it was the satisfaction of Man's ancient necessity to eat in order to survive, but it also seemed to the simple lad from Devon, that it was very much too much for anyone to take home and that, yes, the poor pheasant did not really stand a chance. I knew that these sentiments were unlikely to be very popular in the regiment I was about to join and I enjoyed shooting for the pot, quite enough to buy myself a good double-barrelled 12-bore shot gun as part of my essential kit before going out to Germany.

Just as well that I had because here was a lot of duck to be shot which offended none of my inhibitions, there was also a rarer form of sport provided by the Margrave. Would we like to come to his forests and shoot some wild boar? Well only Punch O'Mara had ever done such a thing but he told us that it was very good sport but also decidedly dangerous; if one did not kill a boar cleanly it was likely to turn round and make a wild charge at its hunter. He had known friends who had only wounded a boar to find that they in turn had been attacked by its immediate charge and had then been badly gored by its tusks. So the first question was what to use to shoot with? The problem was that a bullet from a standard issue Lee Enfield .303 service rifle was likely to go straight through the boar and, unless it destroyed something vital, would pass out the other side without killing it.

The answer provided by Punch, was that there were only two alternatives available to us – we could either use the 12 bore shot-guns we already had, but of course a wild pig would only laugh at 12 bore shot, although it was just right for shooting pheasants because the shot spread as soon as they left the barrel of the gun, and continued their journey as a small cloud, which was much more likely to hit the target than a single bullet. But a cloud of small shot would do a boar no serious injury. However it was possible to take the end off a cartridge, preferably one with heavy shot such as a number 6, then to pour in hot melted wax over the tightly packed shot inside. This would cool rapidly and then the small piece of cardboard might be replaced. The result of all this was that when fired, the shot came out like a solid ball which would burst on striking the boar and do terrible damage. It was still vital, of course, to hit the boar in the chest or side near to its vital organs and then it would stop in its tracks. Well, that was the theory, but Punch said that it worked in practice. The other alternative was to use an issue .303 rifle but to prepare the bullets to be used. These had a very hard cupro-nickel outside case, enclosing a heavy lead core. As designed, the rifle bullet would pass straight through the wall of a house, and equally straight through the boar. However if the end of each bullet were to be filed off, so that the lead core became visible, the effect was similar to the 12 bore cartridge, which had been treated with wax. The bullet would spread on impact and do instant fatal damage to the boar.

I tried both of these methods. Filing off the ends of .303 cartridges was very difficult, but seemed the better possibility if my life and limb were to be at stake. But there was one further difficulty also explained by Punch. One must be careful not to train the rifle in the usual way by putting it up to one's shoulder and using the sites. There would be no time for that. Instead the rifle must be used like a shotgun, when firing at a startled pheasant rising from the ground at the hunter's feet. It must be held close and fired like a pistol from the hip, just by pointing it in the right direction. Well, we knew all about that, but anyway we held a practice run on the firing range just to be sure. I had no moral problems about killing wild boars. It would be very difficult. And anyway it was personally dangerous, and that seemed to make it fair and sporting. There would be a line of beaters coming through the Margrave's forest. The guns had been stationed at different points, out of site of each other so that there was less likely to be any accident. There, in our selected places in the silence of the mighty forest we stood, and we waited, thinking our thoughts, isolated by silence. Hearts beating, listening for the approaching shouts and whistles of the line of beaters, at first distant but slowly getting closer. My eyes were fixed upon that narrow space to my right. There was a bend in the forest to the left. Then suddenly there was a black streak across the ride far to my left. Too far I thought, but I heard the explosion of a nearby shot, and I had just lowered my rifle from my shoulder, when there was a sudden crashing noise, not to my right, but just in front of me and a great black boar burst out and made straight for me. I fired from the hip in the best Western traditions, straight at it. Did I hit it? I was never sure, but if so I certainly did not kill it but it did turn aside and disappeared leaving me scared out of my skin, but not altogether sorry that the splendid panting black beast still lived to roam the Margrave's forest for some time more.

By mid-1947 the wartime army had started to be demobilised. This meant that I had to think of my future. The army were kind enough to suggest that I might like to apply for a regular commission instead of the one I already held which was that of a "War Substantive Lieutenant", in other words not a regular at all but for "hostilities only". But I had no thought of being a regular army officer. Because, of course, I had always known that I wanted to be a latter day Sir Edward Marshall Hall, defender of the difficult cases at the Old Bailey; or at least something like that. So I wrote to the Master of University College at Oxford where I had been an army cadet on a "University Short Course" for six months, some years before. "Could I come back to read Law?" and the answer came back at once that "Yes, you can." So the only problem was to get out of the army as quickly as possible to be there at the start of the next term in October.

Everybody helped me to do just that. The Army had a system of "Class B" release that was for cases just like mine, and I came back to England and went up to York armed with the right papers. Then I was back to being a civilian with my newly issued "demob" suit and the other civilian clothes that a grateful government gave to those who had no other civilian clothes, or at best, ones which were very old and probably much too small. Because clothing was one of the many things still in very short supply in the victorious England of 1947, it was just not possible to buy any new ones without the necessary clothes coupons. I set off for a return to Oxford, to renew some very good friendships I had made three and a half years before. To become fascinated with the study of the law, to play some rugby football, to do some rowing and to drink much too much beer. All of this was at a time when undergraduates at Oxford were not allowed to go to pubs. To be caught was an offence calling for an appearance before the Dean of one's college with the awful possibility of punishment, but the greater likelihood of a reprimand. After all Deans were human themselves and they knew perfectly well that the quaking undergraduate standing before them might well have been a Lieutenant-Colonel in the Commandos a few short months before; so that it was all just a little bit like a descent from the sublime to the ridiculous. And anyway the Dean knew perfectly well that in defiance of the rules almost all undergraduates went into pubs. It was part of the game; part of being "up at Oxford" so that the very worst that was likely to happen was a rebuke. The Dean of my own College did rebuke me but it seemed that the real offence in his eyes was that I had allowed myself to be caught.

The benevolent post-war England helped the returning warrior amazingly. Not only was there a grant available to pay all the University costs of reading law at Oxford but a maintenance grant of £90 a term. It sounds very little now but then it was quite enough to get by quite comfortably at Oxford. The benevolence went on to allowing the returning soldier to "eat his dinners" at his chosen Inn of Court while still at Oxford. So that three times every term there was a need for a trip to London so as to go through the time honoured method of learning a bit about the new profession of being a barrister. Everyone had to eat dinners in hall, in my case the Middle Temple, while doing the Bar Exams. And it was not as silly as it sounds. Eating dinner in the Middle Temple meant meeting other young Bar Students in a "Mess" of four. You were only allowed to speak to the others in your own mess and this meant that you must get to know them. It meant that no one was left out. It meant meeting an interesting mix of fellow students and mature barristers, so that you could discuss your problems, find out the answers and debate about what the law was, what it was going to be and in what respects, if any, you thought that it was all wrong and should be changed.

Barristers have a wonderful tradition of helping the new entrants to the profession and judges and senior members of the Inn would mingle with us and were very ready to talk about any problems. As well as informal discussion there were moots or mock trials, conducted by students "against" more senior barristers and in front of other members of the Inn who might be judges or "silks". Pupillage is an important and enjoyable part of the training of a young barrister. It means that the young hopeful is tucked under the wing of the experienced practitioner, sits at a desk close to his in his Chambers, and follows him about from court to court as he oversees the daily tasks of being a barrister representing all and sundry who can afford his fees; and very

24

often those who cannot but whose case he likes the look of, or who had been granted Legal Aid, or to whom in criminal cases, a Dock Brief or a Poor Prisoner's Defence Certificate had been granted. Any prisoner who asked for one would be granted the right to a dock Brief. This meant that he would come up into court, probably on the first day of the sessions, would make his request and would then be asked to make his choice from any barrister who was present in court. In my early days it cost the prisoner the handsome sum of £1-3s-6d of which £1-1s (one guinea) went to the barrister and the other 2s-6d to his clerk. That was all it would cost him. No matter how long the case might last. The idea was that everyone has a right to be defended when accused of a crime. There was then no other way to pay for the defence of a prisoner accused of a crime which he denied, but who could not otherwise afford to pay the much higher fees that lawyers, instructed in the usual way, would certainly have charged.

The Pearses had been farmers, in the wool trade, merchants, brewers, bankers of the kind they had before the banks all became the present large corporations; they had had some Country Justices and some Ministers of Religion; almost all Methodists since this was the West Country and everyone was a "Methodie". There were even one or two country attorneys and just a very few slightly grander connections with the lesser aristocracy. But no barristers, so that I was striking out into something new and the family looked on in wonder – and predicted the worst. But it is not possible to be an aspiring barrister unless you have self-belief and with very little justification, this is what I had. And I had now passed my Bar Exams in the Inns of Court School of Law at least creditably. Much more importantly I had managed to get a place at 6, Damson Court in the Temple, to do my "pupillage". At that distant time Pupil Barristers were not only paid nothing but even had to pay the Pupil Master 100 guineas for the privilege of getting their coffee, carrying their bag – and learning how it was all done. The young hopeful, is taken under the wing of an experienced barrister and follows him about from court to court, and watches and listens as he does his work. He starts to think "Why did he ask that question?" particularly if it happens that it gets the wrong and rather awkward answer; or "I should have asked something very different – but would that have been any better?"

During his pupillage the young man starts to think for himself. I had had a very good Pupil Master in Wilfred Fordman. He was a very experienced junior, already a Recorder and soon to represent one of the Great Train Robbers in a notable trial. He had the most persuasive way with a jury and even the most apparently hopeless case was not entirely lost if he was for the defence. Exercising defending counsel's prerogative of addressing the jury last he would sum up the apparently damning evidence against his client in his own way. There would be an injection of doubt. Any weaknesses would be ruthlessly exposed. He would end up by saying: "...and members of the jury, what after all does it all amount to? It might look a little bit suspicious... but My Lord, the learned judge... is sure to tell you when he sums up the facts of this case to you, that mere suspicion is not enough. To bring in a verdict of 'guilty' it is essential that you are sure... you must find that guilt has been proved beyond all reasonable doubt."

Of course it did not always work but sometimes it did. And even when it did not, the criminal fraternity admired the efforts that Wilfred put into their cases and his practice flourished. I watched and tried to decide how I could best adapt this technique to my own future forays, into defending those who might come to me in the future. To my great relief Damson Court agreed to take me on as a tenant at the end of my pupillage. So my future at the Bar had started and I was very lucky since they were good "all round" Chambers doing a good mix of both crime, and civil cases involving everything from disputes between neighbours to the occasional more difficult but more lucrative disputes between corporations and financial institutions. They also had connections with the Western Circuit. This was very appropriate for me with Exeter as my hometown. I had relatives and friends there still. I might have no solicitor uncles, but at least our family solicitor had promised he would do what he could to help, by sending me my first few briefs. And of course I knew my way around the West Country.

London was still a strange and unfamiliar place, but there was no other place, for a newly fledged barrister with aspirations to start the difficult process of acquiring a practice. To establish a reputation which would attract clients to come to him rather than to any of the other 1,800 already established barristers, who were his rivals. London was where the Inns of Court were; where most barristers had a "seat" in Chambers; where there were the largest number of solicitors, his potential clients. Time passed and I began to get myself a practice. Some really rather good clients since I had been lucky enough to win some cases and to get some publicity. For reasons connected with my upbringing in Devon I even acquired a nickname "Tam" instead of Francis Pearse. Some wit had remembered the old song about the lending of a grey mare to go to Widdicombe Fair, and the name had stuck. It all helped since many of the best barristers are undoubtedly "characters".

I had been taught, of course, all about the criminal law, including the fact that every sane, adult man or woman, convicted of murder in England, could receive only one sentence. There would be no plea in mitigation. The sentence of the court was inevitable and nothing could change it. I had seen it all being acted out in courts that I attended as a Pupil, with Wilfred Fordman, and sometimes also the head of our Chambers, the redoubtable G.L. Hardy. He was known as "Policeman Hardy" for his fierce cross-examination of police witnesses on behalf of his many clients. Most of these were undoubtedly guilty of the offences with which they had been charged, but still they had a hope of escaping a richly deserved prison sentence, or so they believed, if Hardy was representing them. Because they knew that he, like Wilfred but in a different almost opposite fashion, could often persuade the jury that there still remained a doubt that the police had proved their case. In his case the method was to attack the prosecution evidence, which usually meant an attack on the prosecution's principal witnesses, almost always the police themselves, who he always addressed, regardless of their rank, as "Policeman". When all was lost and the verdict of "guilty" was returned his manner would change and he was persuasive at obtaining lenient sentences if, unhappily he had failed to get an acquittal.

And now I had been in practice for a few years and the number and importance of my solicitor clients was growing but of course, I had never had the handling of that most serious of crimes, murder. However I had been in court when Wilfred had once defended on the "Capital Charge". In such a case, there could be of course be no speech in mitigation of sentence. As soon as the verdict of "guilty" was returned, there would be a brief pause. During this, the judge's chaplain in full vestments, would enter court and sit beside the judge. The judge's clerk would also come in bearing a cushion, and stand beside his judge. At a nod from him, the clerk would take the plain black velvet cap from the cushion and place it on the head of his judge.

Who with the full solemnity of the law, would then intone the dreadful words... "George Herbert Smith... the verdict of this court is that you be taken now...to one of Her Majesty's Prisons and thence... to a place of execution... there you shall be hanged by the neck until you are dead." The chaplain would then intone, with equal solemnity, but with great compassion, "...and may the Lord have mercy on your soul." And the judge would end with finality... "Take him down." The poor wretch would then be led away. Do not say that it was barbaric, although perhaps it was; or that it could not have happened in a civilised country, because it happened here for hundreds of years and in my early days at the Bar it still did. I had already heard it all performed, like some tragedy from the legends of ancient Greece. And wondered...

But by 1961, the Law had started to change. Not to the complete abolition of the death penalty as at present. But, by the Homicide Act of 1957, to a sort of halfway house which created capital murder. This related to just six defined types of murder, for which the only penalty remained a sentence of death. And non-capital murders which were not subject to the death penalty, but which would be dealt with by imprisonment, or if the verdict was "not guilty" of murder but "guilty" of manslaughter, by some lesser penalty such as probation if the facts were very special. Parliament in its wisdom, had decided that among others, murder of a policeman, conviction of a second or subsequent murder, or murder by shooting should remain capital offences, while others should not. This meant as I reflected wryly, when I opened my brief in the case of Regina versus Isabel Jane Earle, and read its contents carefully, that if my client had only, methodically and with premeditation, poisoned her husband, she would not now be in danger of her life. But she

29

had not; she had killed him by shooting him in a fury of temper – or so it was alleged; so that her neck itself was at risk. Of course it all changed long ago and nobody's life is now in danger on conviction for murder of any kind – but then it certainly could be.

My Senior Clerk Challen had the bearing and the manners of a bishop. A week before he had come into my room with a brief in his hands which he had handed to me with a gratified smile. It was a very good case he had assured me, due to start quite soon at the Old Bailey, I would already know about it because he knew that Mr Hawkins had 'phoned me about it several times. And phone me Mr Hawkins certainly had, so that it was really no surprise to me when the brief had finally arrived, but I had still not known for sure that I should get it. Mr Hawkins had a habit of chatting about his cases to me and then, annoyingly briefing some other much more senior barrister to do the case in court. But now it was beyond doubt and Challen knocked at the door and turned to usher in Mr Hawkins of Purvis and Jarrold, that respectable firm of North London solicitors, and Hawkins now took a seat. I knew that he had excelled himself in preparing this case. Henry John Earle the deceased, had been a man with no criminal convictions recorded against him. Yet he was a criminal, and a bad and persistent one at that. He was a "Minder". That was to say he was a friend and an associate of criminals. In particular those who knew of the implications of the criminal law – and the severity of the sentences passed on miscreants found to be in unlawful possession of firearms at that time in history. Those who wanted to use them in the course of their activities or at least to have them handy. They would hesitate to keep them at home in case their house was searched by the police on suspicion of the very offences they were about to commit, but they would be keen to borrow them as occasion demanded. That was where the Minder came in. He would be someone, usually without convictions himself, who would keep firearms safely and lend them out. At a price, of course.

Earle was such a man. He had been married to Isabel Jane, my client for some five years before the events in question. According to friends and neighbours, Mr Hawkins was good at getting the background details, the marriage had been for love; on Isabel's side at least. Earle was tall and handsome. He had never had a proper job but still had a swashbuckling air and disdainful manner. Unfortunately he had a vile and vicious temper as well and the doting Isabel, who was several years younger, was often seen to be bruised in body and down in spirits. Yet still she loved him, apparently, at least. She was the last to know that he had found somebody else. Perhaps her docile nature and devoted ways were not enough for the arrogant, lazy young criminal; for criminal he was. In spite of his lack of convictions for any crime, he merely had not been found out, since of course, it was also an offence to assist others to commit crimes; "Aiding and Abetting" it was called. I read that not content with the attractive Isabel, he had been having an affair with one Irene Barret and this had become intense. Finally he told Isabel that he was leaving her for Irene, who was the wife of a man serving a seven-year stretch and so safely out of the way. The Barrets lived not far from the Earle's North London house at 12, Clacton Street. Mr Hawkins had done his research as well as he possibly could without the advantage of being able to take any instructions at all from the one person who could have told him everything – the client herself.

I had read the graphic account of Mr Hawkins various interviews. He had been very busy indeed, but there was still a glaring gap in the story. Isabel Earle herself had not been able to speak a single word after the events on the night itself on which Henry Earle had been shot dead in his own home. Isabel had been struck dumb. The diligent Mr Hawkins, had busied himself by interviewing every other witness he could get hold of, who could give him an account of the events surrounding the 21st March 1961, the day in question. One witness, a Mrs Elsie Collins, had already volunteered a statement to the police and was happy to find herself able to help Mr Hawkins, with her own graphic account of the events of 21st March.

It had been a dull day at about noon when the neighbours in Clacton Street, N4 had been startled to hear a number of loud shots being fired, with ragged intervals between them. And then, as they rushed startled to their windows, or opened their front doors, the nearby door of number 12, the Earle's house, burst open and Henry Earle had come out, staggered a few yards and collapsed on the pavement. A .45 Colt revolver was seen a few inches from his outstretched hand. And he had stayed where he had fallen, apparently dead. Of Isabel Earle there had been no sign, but when the police were called they had found her in the hallway of her house, sitting on the floor, with her back to the wall, shaken and distressed – and silent. When she was asked what had happened; she had made no reply. She had said not a word to the police at any time since. Not to the police who had first arrived. Not to the woman police constable who had patiently explained her rights to her at the police station. Not to the Metropolitan Magistrate who had asked her, at least to confirm her name at the proceedings before him, when he had committed her for trial to the Central Criminal Court – the Old Bailey. More importantly from my point of view, she had still said nothing at all to Mr Hawkins when he had visited her at

Holloway Prison – Purvis and Jarrold and Co having been assigned by the court to act as her solicitors to defend her – if any defence could be found. The story of what had happened that day was fragmentary and came very largely from the same Mrs Elsie Collins. She had not been present at the dreadful scene. But she had had very little doubt as to what had happened.

"A woman understands another woman, of course, in a way that few men ever can," she had explained. "It was the last straw, Mr 'awkins ...she must 'ave broke... All the rows... we could 'ear them through the wall... all the blows, we could see the marks... she put up with all o' that. But when 'e said 'e would leave 'er... for Irene Barret of all people... well that was it... something broke. She picked up one of 'is guns. Well they was all over the 'ouse. The police found them didn' they? And she just shot 'im, chased 'im, shooting at 'im all the time. Well it's what they say... it was the last straw that broke the camel's back wasn't it? It was the last straw, Mr 'awkins..."

Mrs Collins had no doubt; and for want of any better theory it seemed to be the best explanation. In default of any word from Isabel Earle herself of course, who from first to last had never been able to explain or to excuse the events of 21st March 1961, which would cause her to appear in the dock at the Old Bailey charged for the first time in her life, with a criminal offence – with the capital murder of her husband.

It seemed strange to see Mr Hawkins on his own, in conference at 6, Damson Court. But there was no point in having a silent Isabel Earle in my room. Anyway there would have been serious difficulties since she had, ever since the shooting, been

33

shut up, first in Holloway Prison and later after examination by psychiatrists on behalf of the police, in a secure mental institution awaiting her fate. That did not mean that nothing had been done meanwhile, Mr Hawkins explained. The police had called in their experts. The house in Clacton Street had been thoroughly searched. Bullet marks had been found about the house as well as the two, which had passed through the body of Henry Earle, and the one which had entered his brain and remained there. There was also the one, which had mysteriously passed through the thigh of Isabel herself, causing a painful but superficial injury. All had been photographed. Measurements had been taken and plans drawn. There was a detailed report from Dr. Keith Pinkerton, the leading pathologist of the day. It described the various wounds in detail. And there were also the Depositions.

Depositions are statements in writing of the sworn evidence that the witnesses have given in the Magistrates' Court. They had caused the magistrate at Bow Street to find that a clear prima facie case of murder had been made out against Isabel Earle. Prima facie was the legal jargon meaning "at first sight". Such a case had to be made out, before the expense of jury trial at a place such as the Old Bailey was incurred, and before a defendant was put in peril; in this case of her life. If no such case had been made out so as to satisfy the Magistrates' Court then the matter ended, then and there. A junior member of my own Chambers had attended this hearing but had asked no questions, watching closely to see that everything was in order and reserving the defence for the barrister who was briefed for the trial to decide. In other words I realised with a thrill, non other than me, Tam Pearse. It was essential that the important decisions were made when all the facts were known, and when there had been plenty of time to consider the case made out in the depositions, what the defendant had to say, what the best defence might be and to obtain our own evidence on behalf of the defence. A Prima Facie case had indeed been made out but it was only what it said, "prima facie". There had of course not yet been any testing of the various witnesses by skilful cross-examination. Any probing of the weaknesses and inconsistencies of the prosecution case. That would all be my job at the trial itself.

I turned again to the papers spread before me and read what Dr Pinkerton had to say.

He stated emphatically that there could be no doubt as to the fatal wound. The bullet found to be lodged in his brain would have caused the death of Henry Earle within a matter of seconds, a minute or two at most, of its having been inflicted. The other two had merely passed through his body, without causing serious damage.

Among the papers in my brief there was also a joint report from two psychiatrists, one of whom had the present care of Isabel Earle in her secure institution, and the other, that of the consultant he had referred to. They were agreed that her present condition was caused by the events of 21st March but believed it was so serious that it was irreversible – she was insane and she must have been insane at the time. She should receive treatment urgently now and in all probability it would have to go on for the rest of her life. Then there was the report of the psychiatrist called in by Mr Hawkins. He had consulted me before making his choice and I had had no hesitation in recommending Dr Mary Hambly who was a woman consultant at a London Teaching Hospital. She was also very well known to me since some years before we had become very good friends. A friendship which had included going to a "Commem Ball" at my old college at Oxford. But our brief affair had eventually petered out. We had each to think of the new careers we were just starting. Anyway at the time I could never have afforded marriage, and Mary was far too keen to get a consultancy to allow a romance to interfere with her ambitions. But quite recently we had met again at the Medico-Legal Society where she had been a member for some time and I had more recently joined. On reading her report I saw that she was much more optimistic than the prosecution doctors about the chances for complete recovery of this still young woman.

It had been at my suggestion over the telephone that Mr Hawkins had called her in. Not only because I knew her but because I also knew that she had made a particular study of cases of shell shock and Isabel Earle's condition as explained to me by Mr Hawkins, had reminded me of a case of shell shock that I had come across myself. Mary had clearly become fascinated with the case. Her report showed she was now quite clear about her diagnosis from the description of the incident, and the condition of the patient as she had observed it during her thorough examination. There could be no doubt but that Isabel Earle would not have been entirely responsible for her own actions during the shooting. But she was not insane either then or now, some three months later. Her report went on to explain that there was a rare condition found also as I had guessed in the cases of shell shock in which she had begun to specialise. It would certainly amount to the legal concept of diminished responsibility, she said. Of that, there could be no doubt. But in the opinion of Dr Hambly, it was likely that in time, and perhaps in quite a short time, Isabel Earle would recover her powers of speech and would be able to lead a normal life once more. Her condition was rare but by no means unknown to medical science; it was called hysterical aphonia.

So how to play it? What was the defence going to be? That was what I had to decide and what I discussed at length with Mr. Hawkins. But, of course, in the end the decision had to be mine and I was not yet in a position to take it. Only when I was at court, when all the facts were known, and when I had spoken to counsel for the prosecution, would I be able to decide finally. But the problem was very clear. If Isabel Earle could not speak she could not enter a plea of "guilty" or "not guilty" when the Clerk of the Court read the Indictment to her at the very start of the case. No one else could do it for her. This meant according to Archbold, the great authority on Criminal Law and Practice, that the judge must order that a special jury should be empanelled to decide the single question. "Was she Mute of Malice? – or was she Mute by Visitation of God?" This was the ancient law and, according to Archbold, it was still the right practice. It meant that although there was likely to be no contest on this point at least, much time would be spent on a useless exercise. Nobody had ever suggested that Isabel was "Mute of Malice". This meant that she was staying silent on purpose. I had my own private reservations since I had read the report of Mary Hambly, and I had just wondered if Isabel might not have been faking her apparent complete loss of speech, but none of the experts for the Crown had even suggested such a possibility. However I knew that recently there had been some cases where the Trial Judge had simply taken the easy and very fair alternative of just directing the Clerk of the Court to enter a plea of "not guilty". Nobody could possibly object to that. It was obviously fair to the defendant and it saved a lot of everybody's time and public money. A verdict of "Mute by Visitation of God", had exactly the same effect as a plea of "not guilty" and in view of the prosecution's medical reports that he would have read, it was clearly the right conclusion.

But a plea of "not guilty" meant that the troubles of the defence were only starting. When it was my turn to open the case for the defence; should I call my psychiatrist, Dr Mary Hambly – or should I not? On this decision rested the possible life or death of Isabel Earle, if I did not call her, and lay the foundation for the possible defence of diminished responsibility – then if the prosecution were able to prove their case, she would be found to be guilty and the only sentence possible was that she should hang. As the law then stood, the prosecution could not call medical experts as witnesses, except to rebut or explain medical evidence called by the defence. It was up to me to decide whether or not to do this; to call Mary Hambly to say that it was her opinion that at the time of the commission of the offence, the defendant was suffering from mental illness to such an extent as not really to be responsible for her actions. With the probable consequences of a verdict of "diminished responsibility" so that at least she would not hang; but would be likely to return to the world after a fairly short period of treatment – but with the likelihood that the prosecution would, call their own witnesses with their expressed certainty that at that time the defendant had been "insane within the meaning of the McNaughton Rules" – with the effect that she would be committed to Broadmoor, perhaps to stay there for the rest of her life. So what were the chances that, if I did not call Dr Hambly, the prosecution would not be able to prove their case of capital murder so that she would be able to walk free and start her life afresh?

I looked at the evidence once more. There could be little doubt that Mrs Earle had had the gun in her hands. Or that Earle had died because of a shot from it. Isabel's fingerprints were all over the gun – but then so were those of the deceased. It was his weapon, after all. However the report showed that some of his fingerprints were superimposed over those of the defendant. What did that mean? Did it mean anything? What about the bullet that had passed right through her own thigh? I could not ask Isabel Earle to give me any explanation. But the very facts did raise some interesting possibilities which I might be able to exploit to the jury. The members of it might, after all, be sympathetic to the tragic figure in the dock. There would be likely to be little sympathy for the dead man since everyone seemed to agree that he had been a crook, a bully and a cheat. Mrs Elsie Collins was a witness for the prosecution, but with their knowledge and consent, she had given the statement to Mr Hawkins that I'd read so carefully. It seemed likely that she would be favourable to our case. She had been one of Irene's closest friends. Could I do something with this scant ammunition?

I discussed it with Mr Hawkins. I discussed it with friends and colleagues in my own Chambers. The one person I could not discuss it with was the lady most concerned – who I was never to speak to, never to meet and only to see, for the first time on the first day of the trial, 3rd July 1961. In the end it would have to be my decision and mine alone, a barrister aged only 32, with limited experience of Old Bailey work – and absolutely none of capital murder. Mr Hawkins had rejected any suggestion that the case was so important as to require the services of an experienced Criminal Silk, some Q.C. who had spent many years in the criminal courts.

"No Mr Pearse," he had said, "we don't want any Sir Hartley Shawcross Q.C., thank you. You'll do this case very well. Look what a good job you did for Bernie Lawson, only the other day. I discussed it all with Mr J.C. Purvis my principal, himself. We've got every confidence in you."

"So how do you think we should play it?" I asked. "Should we go for broke and forget about our medical evidence? Go all out for an acquittal? Hope that the jury aren't convinced that she fired the gun at all? Or more likely as I suggest, that there must have been a struggle for the gun, to account for the fact that Henry Earle ended up with it in his hand and that Isabel was shot herself? Because, if so, then it does seem that the possibility of an accidental discharge of the fatal shot could not be ruled out and that must mean that the prosecution have not proved their case and we are entitled to an acquittal?"

"But if we do that we can't call our client to say she did not intend to kill him; that it was all some sort of mistake now can we?" demurred Mr Hawkins, reasonably. And of course he was right. The trouble with going for broke was that we might not succeed and fall flat on our faces. And that would mean the hangman's noose for Isabel Earle. I should have to wait until the last minute to decide. Something unexpected could still turn up. Perhaps a word with the Senior Counsel, who would be conducting the case for the Crown, on the day of the trial might help. It could be that he would let me have the best of both worlds by agreeing that if I called my own medical evidence, which on its own must mean that there would be verdict of manslaughter only because of diminished responsibility, he would not enforce his own right to do the same. If he would only agree to do that, the possibility of a life in Broadmoor for Isabel would be removed. What were the chances that he would not

40

"go for the jugular" and would actually accept that it was rather unfair on any Defending Counsel to have to make such a decision on which the life or death of his client might actually depend? Perhaps I should receive some divine inspiration. I certainly hoped, and prayed, that I should. I eventually made my decision. But I still occasionally wonder, years later, whether the eventual result might have better for Isabel herself, whatever it might have seemed at the time, if I had gone the other way.

Alas! the love of women! it is known
To be a lovely and a fearful thing
For all of theirs upon that die is thrown,
And if 'tis lost, life has no more to bring
To them but mockeries of the past alone,
And their revenge is as the tiger's spring,
Deadly and quick, and crushing, yet, as real.
Torture is theirs, what they inflict they feel.

Don Juan, Canto 2
Lord Byron

Chapter Two

The red bag, made of stout velveteen cloth, and bearing the initials of the barrister in question, is a mark of distinction. It means that he who carries it has, at some time, been Junior Counsel with a Q.C., a "Leader" instructed in the same case, who has been pleased with his preparation, and the help he has been able to give him in court. So pleased that he has bought the red bag in question at Messrs Ede and Ravenscroft, the Legal Robe Makers in Chancery Lane, and had it inscribed with his initials, then to be sent round by his Junior Clerk to the barrister's Chambers. And then to be passed over, with all due solemnity to the recipient's own Senior Clerk. It would have been arranged between them that the lucky recipient would be in Chambers at the time in question, and the two of them would go together to his room to make the presentation. I was myself the proud possessor of a red bag and set off with it over my shoulder with my briefcase in my hand, on Monday 3rd July 1961, out of the Temple through the main gate, then turning right down Fleet Street. I was accompanied by Harold, our Junior Clerk, who now took the red bag. Challen himself had said that he would look in on things later in the morning. It was all a mark of the importance that a case of capital murder had and the brief with the name of the case Rev versus Isabel Mary Earle, on the front of it was such a case. It was still only 9.15 and the case was listed for 10.30, so that we had plenty of time in hand. Time I knew that I needed to find out who was doing the case for the Crown and to talk to him.

I was being trusted by Purvis and Jarrold with this important case, so course I could have no doubts or hesitations myself, the man upon whom the fate of Isabel Earle principally depended. And yet the night before, I had had some doubts... was I after all quite experienced enough for this case? I even mentioned them to Jane, my very pretty young wife of three years. She saw me through very rose tinted glasses it is true, but she restored all the confidence in myself that I usually had; that any barrister has to have. "But darling," she had said with that loving smile which was always so endearing and so comforting, "...of course you will do it beautifully, if anyone can get that unhappy young woman off, then it must be you." I smiled at the memory as we passed El Vino's in the Strand, and then walked across Ludgate Circus, up Ludgate Hill towards St Paul's then left and on to the imposing structure of the Old Bailey. As always it was surmounted, outlined against the sky, by the imposing statuette of Justice. Why was it a woman? Why was she blindfold? Was this perhaps to show the world her lack of corruption and bias? Or was it to acknowledge that because she could not see, just occasionally she got it wrong? She also held in her hand the scales in which she would weigh the all important questions of guilt or innocence, of all the cases being tried within the building stretched below her awe inspiring figure.

Court Number One was reserved for the really important cases. It was presided over by a visiting High Court Judge, the "Red Judge" from the colour of his Judicial Robe, rather than by one of the permanent but lesser judges, who worked there everyday. In this case the judge was to be Henry Scrutton a fairly recently appointed judge, who I had come across at the Bar several times before his appointment to the Bench. There had been publicity about the case, although it was not then realised, that this would be one of the very last cases in which it would be possible for any defendant to be sentenced to death. There was a good crowd already in Court Number One when I made my own entry, having put on wig and gown in counsel's Robing Room. I found that Mr Hawkins was already there. Nothing had changed as far as he was concerned. No new evidence had come unexpectedly to light. Mervyn Griffith was the Senior Counsel for the Crown at the Old Bailey and now he came into court with a solicitor from the Office of the Director of Public Prosecutions, the Senior Clerk from his own Chambers and a young pupil barrister. Now was my chance and I moved across counsel's row of seats and greeted him before asking the vital question.

"Just suppose, because I'm not saying I will, but just suppose that I were to call Dr Mary Hambly as a witness, to found the possibility of diminished responsibility – you will have read her report of course – could you agree to leave it at that? It is your right, of course to apply to the judge for leave to call witnesses in rebuttal, and of course I know from their statements what they would say. But it is only a right and not a duty. You will also know very well that the defence is at a very serious disadvantage in this case. We have no instructions from our client, Mrs Earle. She cannot speak to us anymore than she can speak to anyone else. Your own psychiatric reports show as much. So we don't know what she says really happened at all. I should hate to think that she might be shut up in Broadmoor for the rest of her life almost as much as I hate the thought that she

45

might hang. And you will have read the report of our Dr Hambly?"

"Yes, of course I have."

"It would help redress the balance a bit if you were to agree that in these very odd circumstances, I could call Dr Hambly, and you would not insist on your right to call your own medical evidence, to try to rebut her conclusion that the defendant has hysterical amnesia and is not actually insane at all?"

He paused for thought, and had a brief word with his own instructing solicitor, from the Office of the Director of Public Prosecutions, but only for a moment before saying, "My dear chap, I'm sorry but I don't think I can give any undertakings of that sort on behalf of the Crown. Not in a case of this kind. On any showing she is a danger to the public and ought to be locked up."

"But if I don't call Dr Hambly, then you can't call your medical witnesses either."

"Well, of course as the law now stands that is perfectly right – quite a dilemma for you isn't it? Because there was no one else there and it doesn't look as if he could have shot himself, does it? But then you never know…"

"Wouldn't you agree to accept a plea of guilty of manslaughter?"

"I have already taken instructions on that point from the Director of Public Prosecutions himself, and I am sorry but the answer is 'no'."

So there it was. There was going to be no easy way out for me, or for Isabel Earle for that matter. At that moment there was a sound from the dock and I turned and looked round, in time to see two hefty women wardresses enter, bringing a small forlorn-looking figure between them. For a moment she stood, wearing a drab prison dress, of the kind that I had previously seen on the inmates of Holloway Prison; it did nothing to improve her appearance, but it could not conceal her slim figure and rather haunting beauty. She appeared to take little interest but just before she sat down she did look round the court and looked for a moment at Mr Hawkins, who of course she had met, and who was sitting just behind me. Then she looked directly at me and met my own interested gaze. She looked even younger than the 27 I knew her to be. Her face had no trace of make-up upon it. Of course they were not allowed anything of that kind in secure mental institutions. I thought that she looked aware of where she was. I guessed that somehow she was aware of what was going on, but did this sad little person realise how much of her fate rested on the young barrister who was to defend her? Who she was probably never destined to meet, and who she could not ask "Oh, please do your best for me?" I did not know and never could. But of course I was going to do my best for her anyway, it was by far the most important case I had ever had.

At that moment there was a stir in court as the usher came importantly in, calling "All rise for the Queen's Justices" and, as everyone dutifully rose to their feet, in came a little group consisting of the Sheriffs of the City of London, who were responsible for proceedings at the Old Bailey, the judge's clerk and his chaplain, and finally the red-robed figure of Henry Scrutton. The judge was conducted to his ornate seat appropriately higher up than anyone else's, and duly sat upon it. Everyone else sat down as well at this signal and the retinue, having bowed once more to the judge, duly went out, their duties at an end until they attended him again to conduct him out of court to have his lunch. The judge addressed the Clerk of the Court who was standing looking at him expectantly. The defendant alone, with the wardresses on either side of her, had also remained standing.

"Let the Indictment be put to her," said the judge and the clerk turned to the prisoner saying, "Isabel Jane Earle, you stand here on an Indictment which charges you with capital murder, in that on 21st March of this year you did kill Henry John Earle by shooting him. How say you … are you guilty, or not guilty?"

And everyone looked expectantly at the small figure in the dock. But she just stayed quite silent looking to her front, there was no sound in court; until at last the judge said, "Put the Indictment to her again." And so it was. But the result was just the same.

"Mr Griffith, Mr Pearse," said the judge and we both rose respectfully to our feet, "I have read the depositions in this case and the various medical reports. Although they may differ as to the severity and the effect of the defendant's mental condition, I think that they leave no doubt that the defendant's present silence in answer to the charge, is as a result of that condition, so that there can be no doubt but that her silence is not as a result of any malicious intent on her part?"

We both agreed.

"So I shall direct that a plea of 'not guilty' be entered," ordered the judge. "Let a jury be sworn."

Then there were the formalities to be completed according to the tradition of all criminal trials by jury. The Clerk of the Court rose to his feet and called for the jury-in-waiting, who came into court to take their seats, with all the dignity they could muster for the importance of their position that day. Each in turn stood up and, taking the bible, or in one case the Koran, in his or her right hand, read from the card the usher presented to them:

"I swear by Almighty God to duly try the several issues joined, between Her Sovereign Majesty the Queen and the Prisoner at the Bar, to harken to the evidence and true verdict make." Looking a little embarrassed each then took his or her seat and looked about them, and at the prisoner in the dock with special interest. I sat silent while all of this was going on. I had a right to challenge any member of the jury "as he or she came to the book to be sworn and before he or she was sworn." I had no need to give any reason, for seven challenges, and then I could make any number I liked if I could "show cause" why some particular would be juror should be disqualified. If perhaps he or she knew the defendant or any of the other witnesses. But if I did make a challenge it would mean that that juror had to stand aside and another would take his place. Some counsel for the defence took the view, I knew, that for a female defendant it was better to have an all male jury. The reasoning being that it was thought that women were less sympathetic to another woman and men more so. The number of "Challenges without Cause" allowed would mean that it was possible to obtain an all male jury by challenging all women jurors, merely because they were women, until a jury composed entirely of men remained. I had thought about this, but I knew that Challenges without Cause, as they were called, might rebound a bit. The jury might ask themselves what it all meant and would be unlikely to find any satisfactory answer. They might wonder what trick was being played on them and react against the instigator of it – the defence. So I kept my seat until the last of them sat down and the Clerk of the Court asked, superfluously but traditionally, "Members of the jury are you all sworn?" expecting and receiving, no answer to his question.

Then the defendant was formally "put in the charge of the jury", the clerk saying with all due solemnity, "Members of the jury, the defendant is charged on Indictment that on 21st March she committed capital murder causing the death of Henry John Earle by shooting him. To this Indictment, by direction of the judge, a verdict of 'not guilty' has been entered. Now it is your duty to harken to the evidence and then to say whether she be guilty or not."

And the clerk took his seat. "Yes, Mr Griffith?" said the judge courteously and Counsel for the Crown duly started to make his opening address to the jury.

"May it please you, My Lord, in this case I appear for the prosecution and my learned friend, Mr Francis Pearse appears for the defence." He then recited the facts very fairly. After all, I thought cynically, they looked damning enough; there was no need for embroidery. There was the stark fact that on a quiet afternoon in Clacton Street, shots had suddenly been heard; fired close together but at uneven intervals. After a few moments of silence, the door of Number 12 had burst open and the defendant's husband had staggered out, and taken a few lurching paces, before falling dead on the pavement. The neighbours at once called the police but the only person to be found in the house when they arrived was the defendant, the dead man's wife, now his widow. She had never given any explanation at all as to what had occurred and she was the only person now alive, who possibly could. The jury might hear in due course, certain medical evidence which could amount to some sort of explanation for the defendant's conduct that day. The prosecution could not say that they would hear such evidence because that was a matter for the defence. He paused and looked at me invitingly. But I was not going to commit myself until I had to, and knew that I should have to make the most difficult decision of all soon enough.

"It will be a matter entirely for you, members of the jury," said Mervyn Griffith. He stood hands on hips, and allowed himself a complacent smile, he knew that the best cards lay in the hands of the prosecution that day, "...but the case for the

Crown is that, although there is no direct evidence as to what occurred, the inference that it was this defendant who shot and killed her husband is, in the view of the prosecution quite irresistible – look at the facts. Shots are heard. The only people in the house are this man and this woman, a husband and wife known to be on bad terms with each other. There is no doubt about the cause of death, no doubt about the weapon which was used. It was found near the outstretched hand of the deceased man outside his own house. The defendant's finger prints are upon the gun and I shall call before you forensic expert witnesses from New Scotland Yard, who conducted tests upon the defendant shortly after she was taken into custody that day. These will prove, beyond doubt you may think, that she had recently fired a gun. You may think also that there can be no real doubt that it was this gun that she had fired." And he held up the Colt .45 revolver Exhibit 1 in the case, pausing for a moment for dramatic effect, "...you will also hear that the bullet which entered the brain of the deceased and caused his almost instant death, had been fired from this same weapon. It is sad, members of the jury, because the killing of a husband by a wife must always be sad, whatever provocation there may have been, but at the end of the day the prosecution will ask you to say that you must honour the oaths you have sworn and that there is only one verdict that you can possibly return." He did not need to say what he thought that verdict would be and resumed his seat before calling the first witness for the Crown.

The case went on with the calling of one witness after another. The police officers who had been called to the scene spoke of the crowd which had already gathered round the ambulance men, who were lifting the body onto the stretcher on its way to the mortuary. Then there were the officers who had made a meticulous examination of the house and noted the exact positions of five bullets out of the six which, it was said that the Colt .45 would have contained if fully loaded that day. It seemed that it must indeed have been fully loaded. Of the six in question, two could be identified as having passed through the body of the deceased and one, that was the strange thing, had evidently passed through the body of the defendant herself since it bore minute traces of her blood which was of a different group from that of her husband. And the sixth bullet had been removed from the brain of the dead man, and it too had certainly been fired from a Colt .45 which must have been the same revolver. None of this was in dispute. They were all undoubted facts and I could only sit and watch and listen since there was no scope for brilliant cross-examination here. It was the same with Dr Keith Pinkerton, the pathologist. There was nothing which I could dispute about his careful and knowledgeable account of his examination of the body in the mortuary, and his conclusion that the cause of death was the single bullet still found in his body, the one in his brain. This would have caused, Dr Pinkerton was clear, his almost instant death.

I rose to my feet to cross-examine. There was little I could dispute. But might I be able to sow any seed of doubt at all in the minds of the jury?

"Dr Pinkerton, from what you have said, about the fatal wound being the almost instantaneous cause of death, it must follow mustn't it, that the deceased could have fired it himself?"

"That is not for me to say," he replied, as I had thought that he would.

"But the weapon in question was found, was it not, close to his outstretched hand on the pavement outside his house?" I persisted

"So I have been told."

52

"And doesn't that mean that if he had had it in his hand a few seconds before his death, he might have squeezed the trigger himself just possibly on purpose, but perhaps even more likely by accident? Or perhaps, since the defendant received a wound herself that day, that there might have been a struggle for the gun during which she received her wound – and the deceased himself, received the fatal wound?"

"That does seem just possible, but it is certainly not for me to speculate."

"Well, I think that that is exactly what the prosecution are asking the jury to do in this case?"

Dr Pinkerton remained silent. But I had made a point and I sat down feeling just a flicker of hope. It did not seem at all possible that Henry Earle would have had the slightest desire to kill himself. He was just about to go off and leave his wife for some other woman whose charms could only be guessed at. But might it all have been an accident? There was that unexplained and mysterious wound to the thigh of the defendant herself to be accounted for; if it ever could be, I mused.

"Call Mrs Collins," said Mervyn Griffith and I looked up with interest to see a short busy-looking lady with blonde hair, recently permed I thought, with perhaps just a shade too much peroxide, enter the court and head towards the witness box in a determined manner. Up in the public gallery a small group of women of about the same age and general appearance as the new witness, leaned forward for a better view, and I thought with wry amusement, that the friends of Elsie Collins must have come to court for a day out. To see their neighbour have her hour of glory. Their hairdressers too seemed to have been doing good business, I noticed. When she had been sworn in Mervyn Griffith elicited from her the story of that afternoon in Clacton Street. The housework done, Mrs Collins had been putting her feet up with the newspaper and a cup of tea. Then out of her moment of peace and quiet, had come "like a bolt from the blue" she said, "a series of loud explosions". She had never heard a shot fired before but that's what they must have been, she was sure. So she had rushed to her own front door and opened it to gaze fearfully into the familiarity of Clacton Street. At first nothing had happened but after a pause, there was one further shot and then the door of Number 12 burst open. Henry Earle came staggering out, and lurched up the street away from her before falling prostrate on his face. Stretched out on the pavement, said Elsie Collins, "for all the world like 'e wos a piece a meat laid out on th' slab o' a butcher's shop." Elsie's graphic turn of phrase was rising to the occasion and evoked, I noticed, a murmur of quiet approval from her group of friends in the public gallery.

Now it was my turn and I rose to cross-examine, looking down at the statement that Mr Hawkins had obtained for me from Mrs Collins:

"You say that there were pauses between the firing of the various shots?"

"Yes, I do."

"And these were of uneven duration, so that perhaps, in the moments of silence the two people within the house had moved from room to room?"

"Yes, perhaps he was trying to get away…"

"Or, perhaps, it was she… our friend Irene, I reminded her "…who was trying to get away from him, chasing her with one of his own weapons, smoking in his hand?"

"Yes, I s'pose that could 've been it – could 'ave been 'er 'oo was tryin' to get away," she conceded.

"And equally likely, don't you think… remember that there were two bullets found in the house, in different rooms, which

54

were found to have no traces of blood, which could have been fired by either Henry or Isabel Earle... remember Mrs Collins, that the fingerprints of both the defendant... and her husband... were found on that Colt .45 pistol?"

"Yes, it could 'ave been either of 'em 'oo was doing the shootin'," agreed Elsie Collins, warming to her theme and recognising the possible benefit for her friend. "I couldn' possibly tell... 'ow could I?"

"And I think that you had some reason to believe that Henry Earle was going to tell her that he was leaving her that day?"

"Well I 'ad 'eard... on good authority... it was from my Bert, who 'ad it from George Barret down at the pub. You mustn't think that Bert usually goes round with that lot down there." Elsie Collins looked up to her friends in the gallery to be sure that they had noted the point. "...but 'e did just 'appen to drop in when George Barret was in there 'aving a drink. That's George Barret 'oose brother Dick, was sent down for a long stretch for robbery," explained Mrs Collins. "...'oose wife Irene, was always a bit of a ..." Elsie remembered where she was just in time, "slag" was a word she knew that she shouldn't say, not under the glare of the spotlight of giving evidence at the Old Bailey, "...well anyway, Irene got a bit tired o' waitin' and 'ad been friendly for quite some time with 'Enery Earle. Well you could say very friendly," she paused for a moment to see what effect this would have upon her audience. She looked up at the judge but he only allowed a brief smile of encouragement to cross his features. "...well it seems that George 'ad 'eard from 'is brother, that Irene had told 'im, that she was going off with 'Enery Earle to start a new life t'gether. That she 'ad given in 'er notice to the Council for the 'ouse they 'ad in Ernshaw Street, an' that 'Enery was going to tell Isabel, an' clear out all 'is

55

things on Friday... well it was on Friday, that it all 'appened wasn't it?" said Elsie Collins, it was irrefutable. And then she repeated what she had already told Mr Hawkins and said with all the conviction of a woman who knows she is right:

"Well, 'e knocked 'er about. We could all see the marks often enuff. But she stood by 'im didn't she? She loved 'im, rogue that 'e was, but when 'e told 'er 'e was going to leave 'er for another woman, and for Irene Barret of all people, that was too much. It was the straw that broke the camel's back – the last straw."

"And as for Isabel Earle herself, your friend I know, she had put up with it all, more than many another woman would have, and was still a good and loving wife to him?"

"Yes, she stood by 'im thro' thick an' thin even tho'..."

And Mrs Collins paused uncertainly.

"Yes? Even though what?"

"Well there was one bloke 'oo seemed to fancy 'er a lot. A young bloke, I don' think 'e was from our part... but quite 'andsome a'most a gent I'd say. But she saw 'im off a treat. I 'eard 'er say to 'im Mr Fortescue, you clear off I'm 'appily married, thank you all the same and clear off 'e did, then 'an there."

"So she gave him no encouragement at all and you never saw him again?"

"No, I did'n', well not to be sure.... altho' I did think once, I saw someone a bit like Mr Fortescue comin' out of 'er 'ouse late one night. But I must 'ave been mistaken, 'cos when I 'ast 'er she said she hadn't seen 'im since."

Elsie Collins had the look of quiet satisfaction of a woman who has done her duty. A woman who has managed to tell the court the true facts. A court which otherwise would have been left in sublime ignorance. She clearly thought that she had

56

managed to explain the mysteries of the female sex to the unsympathetic masculine world.

Of course a great deal of the evidence had been what the lawyers call "hearsay". Objection could have been taken to a lot of it by Mervyn Griffiths. But none had been. The judge himself had said no word of protest. There was, everyone realised, simply no other way for the court to hear of the all-important tittle-tattle of Clacton Street, than from the mouth of one of the neighbours. The main witnesses to it all could not be called to give evidence. Henry Earle was dead. And Isabel…? I looked across at the pale, silent figure in the dock. Was she taking it all in and understanding it? It was her life that was at stake. We all knew so little about her that I thought that I would do my best to fill it all out for the jury with the only person that I could. The garrulous Mrs Collins who was certainly no-body's fool and someone the jury might understand and sympathise with. She was turning now, about to leave the witness-box but I stopped her, anxious to get the very best I could from a sympathetic witness.

"She was your friend, wasn't she, Mrs Collins?"

She nodded emphatically.

"What sort of person was she? Had you ever known her to have bouts of violent temper, as the prosecution would have us all believe she did that day last March?"

"She was a good friend to me and I certainly never 'eard 'er in a temper," affirmed Mrs Collins earnestly. "…we'd go to the pictures t'gether. She was a really nice person. We'd 'ave a good gossip sometimes, but she wouldn't speak badly o' no one – certainly not ag'inst 'im, 'er 'usband. She was quite superior too, spoke just like they do on the BBC. Didn't come from round 'ere at all – but I don't know where she did come from neither."

Well that description did fill out the defendant a bit. It did give did her just a bit of a personality, I thought. There followed the last witness for the prosecution. The officer in charge of the case, Detective Chief Inspector Hollingsworth who had arrived at the scene soon after the body had been taken away. He explained that the weapon concerned could contain only six cartridges, and that in fact it seemed that it had, and that all six were accounted for. He went on to explain his various meetings with the defendant and that during all of them she had remained silent. When he had charged her he had used the time-honoured formula, "Isabel Jane Earle I charge you with the murder of Henry John Earle, by shooting him... you need say nothing in answer to the charge... but anything you do say will be taken down in writing and may be used in evidence at your trial... do you wish to say anything?" And she had said nothing. And I, when my turn came, had almost nothing to ask the last witness for the prosecution. I had no case to put to him for the defendant, because of course she had said nothing to Mr Hawkins. There was nothing for me to challenge or to disagree with, in anything he had said. If she had a case at all, then I should have to invent it by my own theory of what might have happened that day in North London.

So I rose to my feet and asked, "What about the wound to the defendant's thigh Chief Inspector? We have heard very little about that?"

"Well, Sir, there is not much to say. The bullet in question had just passed through the fleshy part of the thigh. It was treated by the ambulance men, at the scene and later examined by the doctor at the police station. It was a clean wound and healed up quite quickly."

"The body heals more quickly than the mind Chief Inspector?"

"I couldn't say, Sir."

"Perhaps not, but could you determine which shot it was that caused the injury to the defendant, the first or the last, or which?"

"All I can say Sir, is that it was probably not the last shot that was fired because this shot was found lodged in the wall of the hall. It had faint traces of her blood upon it. She was Group AB and he was Group O. It seems certain that there was a shot or shots fired after the one that wounded the defendant."

"And the weapon itself was found with all six cartridges fired, and close to the outstretched right hand of the deceased on the pavement outside Number 12, wasn't it?" I reminded the Chief Inspector and he agreed that it had been.

"And you can't really be sure, can you Chief Inspector, that it was not the deceased's own finger that was on the trigger when the fatal shot was fired?"

"Well it's not really for me to say Sir," said the Chief Inspector, once more. But he somehow managed to make it plain, how unlikely it was that Henry Earle had committed suicide, with a new affair with Irene Barret about to begin. And I was afraid that the jury might think so too.

"And equally you could not really be sure that the shot that killed Henry Earle, probably it was the last shot of all, was not fired just after the shot which went through the defendant's thigh. In the course of the same struggle for the gun and equally by mistake? By an accident?"

"It does not seem very likely, Sir."

"But you could not rule it out altogether now could you, Chief Inspector?"

But he did not answer and I decided not to press him and sat down, satisfied that I might just have sewn a seed of doubt – if the jury were sympathetic, as well they might be.

The prosecution then went on to call their own police evidence as to what had happened that day after they had arrived at the scene. Their meticulous examination of the house and the positioning of the various bullet holes and then, "That is the case for the prosecution, My Lord," said Mervyn Griffith so that at last it was my turn.

"Yes Mr Pearse?" said the judge as I rose to my feet:

"My Lord, as we are all by this time only too painfully aware I am in no position to call my client to give her own account of her life with the deceased, and of the happenings of Friday 21st March of this year, and the events which led up to them. I shall be calling medical evidence to show that if the jury should be satisfied at the end of the day, that the death of the deceased was caused by the wilful and intentional act of the defendant, then at that time her mind was so unbalanced that she was not fully responsible, that she had diminished responsibility for her actions."

The judge interjected, "And if you do take that course, Mr Pearse, it will mean of course that if he wishes, Mr Griffith can apply to me for leave to call his own psychiatrists to give evidence – whose reports I know you will have considered carefully?"

"Yes, My Lord," I replied, "…I have given the matter very careful thought… and I call Dr Mary Hambly."

And so the die was cast. Mary Hambly took her place in the witness-box, was duly sworn, and gave her evidence that she had no doubt that Isabel Earle was suffering from hysterical aphonia at the time, the meaning of which she explained carefully. She went on to explain that it meant that the defendant was not really responsible for her actions at the time in question. Even if she had deliberately fired at Henry Earle, any usual presumption that she had meant to kill him, would not apply to a woman in a condition which was similar in medical terms to the cases of shell shock which she had treated, and on which subject she was the author of a medical treatise. If acceptance of this opinion, resulted in a verdict of "not guilty" to murder, but "guilty of manslaughter" as she believed that it might, then medical treatment would be helpful. A full recovery at some future time was almost certain.

But that was not the end of the matter, unfortunately for Isabel Earle, although I still held high hopes that the prosecution could never make out their charge of capital murder anyway, since surely they could not exclude the possibility of it all having been a tragic accident during the course of a frantic struggle for the gun? The application by the prosecution to call their own medical witnesses could not be resisted. And they duly appeared and gave their own evidence.

Not for the first time, and certainly not for the last, I discovered that eminent, well-qualified professional men, doing their best no doubt to assist a court of law to arrive at the correct conclusion, could take a view quite different from an equally eminent colleague. Mrs Earle, in their considered view, had not been responsible for her actions that day; so far they could agree with Dr Hambly their distinguished colleague, but it went further, much further than that. Mrs Earle, in their considered opinion was insane within the meaning of the McNaughton Rules. These rules, had been in force since the early days of Queen Victoria. They had been introduced into the law in cases of murder as a novel act of mercy, which would sometimes prevent a convicted defendant from being hanged. If a defendant were to be found to have been guilty but that at the time he either did not know what he was doing, or did not know that it was wrong, then the correct verdict for the jury to bring in was "guilty but insane". It would mean that the defendant would be

61

sent to a "secure mental institution", probably Broadmoor, and quite often would stay there for the remainder of his or her life. For the still young, rather pathetic rather beautiful, figure in the dock it was an awful fate to contemplate – but not so bad a one after all, I reflected, as that she should be hanged by the neck until she was dead, which could have been her fate if I had not opened the door to medical evidence by calling Dr Hambly Hambly. And after these distinguished doctors had given their evidence, politely but definitely contradicting that of Dr Hambly, that was the end of the evidence. The last witness for the prosecution had been called.

"Would that be a convenient moment to adjourn?" said Mr Justice Scrutton rhetorically, as he rose to his feet and made for the way out to the judicial corridors behind the court. So it was all over for the day and I should be able to open the case for the defence in the morning – and I had that night to reflect on what I should say, because I had no defendant nor any other witness to call on her behalf.

The next morning as 10.30 approached, found me sitting in my place in Court One, waiting for the judge to come in and for the proceedings to begin for the day. The jury were already in their places and I glanced at them. Eight good men and true and four women, who would between them decide the great issue of the day, but our start that day was delayed as one of them had been ill in the night and arrived late. They had all been listening apparently with great care. One in the front row, a young woman of about Isabel's age and general appearance, wearing a pink summer dress, more suited perhaps for Wimbledon or Ascot than for the dusty corridors of a criminal court, had seemed to be listening with particular attention, and even perhaps to have displayed a trace of emotion herself, as Elsie Collins had described the events which had taken place, in her belief, inside

Number 12 Clacton Street between husband and wife on that morning in March. Perhaps I should keep my gaze on her, since I could not look at all twelve of them at once. It might be all in my imagination, but she seemed to have a sympathetic eye. Then we all rose to our feet as the judge made his ceremonial entry. A glance at the dock showed that the defendant was in her place, flanked by her attendant, rather grim-looking, wardresses and looking as usual straight ahead, her eyes not seeming to focus on anything or anybody. Her mind perhaps not really in Court One at all but in some quite different place, and some remote period of her past. Perhaps some time when she was first very much in love with Henry Earle I wondered, as a faint smile momentarily played about her mouth.

I stood up again and opened my defence with the time-honoured words: "may it please you M'Lud... members of the jury, you have already been told by my learned friend for the prosecution, and I am sure that you will be told again by My Lord when summing up the facts of this case to you and directing you on the law, that it is for the prosecution to prove that the defendant is guilty and not for her to prove that she is not. As the lawyers say, the onus is upon them not upon her. And the charge is murder. Which means a wilful intentional act. Intentional in the sense that the defendant must have not only fired the shot which killed her husband, but must also must have really meant to kill him that day. Or at least not to have cared whether he died or not. That must all be proved for you beyond any reasonable doubt, in order for you to find her 'guilty'. You would have had to exclude every other possibility with certainty. And every one of you would have to be agreed about it.

"Never mind that she may have had good reason to wish him dead, in view of the way he had behaved towards her and what he may have said... and how do we really know if in fact

63

he did… about his affair with Irene Barret. Never mind theory or supposition, suppose instead that we just concentrate on the facts. The things we really know about that day. That we can be sure of, as the law says we must be sure, in any case of this gravity. Six shots were fired; that we know. One of them killed the deceased man. That one must have been the last that was fired since Dr Pinkerton has told us that Henry Earle would only have lived for a matter of seconds after receiving it in his brain. The others were all fired within the house; that we can be sure of. But who by? And aimed at whom or what? This is where the facts we can be sure of end, and supposition begins, you may think members of the jury and it is for you, and only you, to say. The prosecution has asked you to say that you can be sure that it was the defendant who fired the shots and that her intention can only have been to kill her husband. They say that this is the overwhelming and only real, inference that you can draw. And that having drawn it you should bring in a verdict of 'guilty of capital murder'.

"But isn't that forgetting one thing? One very important thing, you may think? Something about which we have heard very little. Something which the prosecution is unable to explain and so it hasn't tried to. Something that has really been glossed over, but which I suggest, and it is for you to judge, may be the most important thing in the whole case? The defendant received a shot from that same Colt .45 pistol, through her own thigh. How did she get that? It is quite unexplained. I have already made the suggestion in cross-examination to the Detective Chief Inspector and he could not discount it. Might it not have been that at some point these two had a struggle for possession of the gun? Inside the house, of course, and almost certainly between the first and the last shots that were fired, probably the last but one. Perhaps, who knows? The defendant did take up one of her

64

husband's deadly weapons, perhaps there was a chase and shots were fired, then the struggle. During it the deceased seized his own revolver, were both their hands upon it at the vital moment? And then it went off again. Once to send a shot through the defendant's thigh – and once more to send the shot through his own brain?

"When you are considering this matter quietly in your room and deciding what your verdict is going to be, members of the jury" ... I paused and looked into the eyes of the young woman in the pink dress. She was certainly listening intently, whether it was with sympathy or not, it was hard to say, "...I ask you to remember these two things particularly... firstly the wound in the defendant's thigh... ask yourselves how it was caused? Might it not even have been that when that vital shot was fired, it was only the finger of the deceased that was on the trigger? The second is the fact that the weapon which did all the damage was afterwards found close to the dead man's outstretched hand as he lay dead on the pavement outside – while my client, the defendant remained inside her own house, shocked and shaken. Doesn't that mean that he probably seized the weapon from the defendant? That there was indeed some struggle for possession? Perhaps the gun went off during the struggle and caused the wound in the defendant's thigh? By accident? Perhaps it went off again as he was wresting it from her, near the front door which burst open? Again by accident? And that that was the shot which killed? Doesn't it all fit in and show that this theory is the correct one? But the really important question for you is this one... can you really be sure that that could not have happened? That it could not all have been an accident?

"The prosecution concede that there is no direct evidence in this case. That it is all a matter of inference and they say that the proper inference for you to make is that the defendant killed her husband by shooting him and that it was intentional but... before we get to any possible consideration of the conflicting medical evidence we have heard... because if you cannot exclude the possibility that Henry Earle's death could have been an accident, then you cannot possibly convict Isabel Earle of murder and your verdict must inevitably be... not guilty. So you do not need to consider the conflicting medical evidence at all. The case of murder would not have been proved. Your only proper verdict would be one of 'not guilty' and this young woman would go free to try to pick up the threads of a life shattered by tragedy; marred by her love for the husband who had betrayed her so constantly.

"If however, in spite of all the uncertainties, you are convinced beyond reasonable doubt, that the defendant did kill her husband as an intentional and deliberate act, then you will have to go on to consider the conflicting medical evidence. I suggest that you prefer that of Dr Hambly. The only medical witness with particular experience of cases of shell shock, the symptoms of which she told you were so similar to the symptoms now displayed by Isabel Earle. She told you that she is quite sure that the defendant is suffering only from hysterical aphonia. And is not insane at all. You will remember, that the evidence of the prosecution itself is that she was silent from the very first moment after the tragic events in question... everyone is agreed that she has not said a single word from that day to this. It would mean, Dr Hambly is clear about it, that she had a diminished responsibility for her actions so that your verdict would be one of 'not guilty of murder but guilty of manslaughter'. It is only if you reject the clear view expressed by Dr Hambly that you would have to conclude that she was in fact insane within the meaning of the McNaughton Rules and in that event she would inevitably be sent to Broadmoor – perhaps for the rest of her life. Do you really think that she is insane and was so at the time? Without even hearing her own account from her, since she is unable to give it? Just pause for a moment and think of the account you have heard from Mrs Elsie Collins. Her description of her friend as a good companion, fond of a gossip and going to the pictures together – does that sound to you like a young woman who was mad?"

I paused for several moments just looking at the young woman in the pink summer dress. And Court One of the Old Bailey remained totally quiet until I sat down feeling rather pleased with myself. A bit of an appeal to reason as I saw it and to the emotions as well, might just do the trick? At least I had tried to sow the seed of doubt in the minds of the jury which would lead to acquittal for Isabel Earle. And as I resumed my seat I glanced up at the lady herself. There she sat immobile between the wardresses, ready at any moment to restrain her from any rash move to attack the judge or to try to escape the inevitable hand of justice. She was motionless as usual, no expression on her face, no sign of understanding. Did she realise that her life was in danger? It seemed not. But then she turned for a moment to look directly at me. Our eyes met and… just for a brief second, did a faint smile flit across her face? Did her right eye drop for half an inch in a furtive wink? I could not be sure and stared at her fixedly but once more she was sitting quite motionless. There was no expression at all upon her pale, lovely face.

Mr Justice Scrutton began his summing up at once. He went through all the evidence with meticulous care. He directed the jury that to find the defendant guilty of capital murder they must firstly be sure that when she had fired the fatal shot, she intended to kill her husband. Or even to maim or wound him; that would be enough. If she fired recklessly or not caring whether she killed him or not, that would still be sufficient. Then he went on briefly; much too briefly for my liking, to deal with the need for certainty in view of the possibility that had been put before them by the defendant's counsel, that in spite of all the obvious appearances, the actual death might have been caused by some accidental pulling of the trigger which fired the fatal shot. At a time when both their fingers were on the trigger of the gun perhaps, or even conceivably, because counsel had asked them to consider this, only the finger of the dead man himself. They should consider this, of course, because it was the Crown's duty to prove their case. But the judge spent little time on my own favoured view of the matter, which I really had come to believe myself was a possible, if not the probable answer. And when he did so, the well-known Scrutton sneer was very obvious. No one listening could possibly misunderstand that the judge himself did not believe a single word of it.

He went on to elaborate on the possibility of a verdict of guilty of manslaughter instead of murder. This would be correct if their conclusion was that she had fired the gun, but that her intention had been, not to cause his death but merely to wound or injure him. It was a fine distinction for any jury to have to make, I thought, because he had just told them that if she had been reckless as to the consequences not caring if she killed him or not, then that would still be murder. He continued by saying that, if satisfied that the defendant had wilfully caused the death of her husband, then they should go on to consider the medical evidence which had been called before them both by the defence, and then but only because counsel for the defendant had first done so, also by the prosecution. They should consider the whole of it. If at the end of the day they accepted the evidence of the two eminent psychiatrists called by the prosecution, who had been quite satisfied that at the time of the commission of the offence, she had been insane within the meaning of the McNaughton Rules, then their correct verdict would be "guilty of murder but insane". If however they rejected that evidence and accepted instead the evidence of Dr Mary Hambly that although not insane the mind of the defendant was affected at the time in the way she had described, so that her responsibility for the awful acts was diminished, then they would return a verdict of "guilty of manslaughter by reason of diminished responsibility".

"It is now not yet time for the adjournment," said the judge looking up at the clock above him, "but I have other business to attend to and I shall finish my summing up tomorrow, members of the jury, rather than now. This means that you can go off home for the day. Once I have finished my remarks to you the defendant will be put in your charge and you must not then speak to anyone who is not a fellow member of the jury, or the Court Jury Bailiff, until you have delivered your verdict, so that if I did finish now, then you would have to stay together, until you had reached your verdict and the case had concluded."

And so we all rose for the day. When we came back next morning the judge concluded by saying, "Members of the jury, remember to put out of your minds anything you may have read about this case in the newspapers. Or anything at all which other people may have said to you about it. In particular you must exclude from your minds any opinion as to 'guilt' or 'innocence' that anyone else may have expressed to you. Even if it be your spouse or some other member of your own family. You must judge it all by what you have heard in this court and nothing else." And then the Jury Bailiffs were duly sworn, "To well and truly keep this jury and suffer no one to speak to them without the leave of the court. Nor to speak them ourselves save to enquire if they be agreed upon their verdict." The jury went out to begin their deliberations and I went off to the refreshment room with Mr Hawkins for a well-deserved cup of coffee. When Mr Hawkins and I had finished our coffees, in came Mervyn Griffiths and sat down beside us.

"So Tam, what do you reckon your chances are?" he asked.

"Well I think that there is quite enough doubt about it all for her to get the benefit of it – and be acquitted. And so I think she should be," I said stoutly.

"What with all that blood and all those shots being fired?" he mused dubiously. "It's true of course that he was a very bad lad indeed and no one is going to miss him much. Except for Irene Barret of course, but I'm afraid there's not much doubt that your client is as guilty as hell... the sooner she's locked up for good the better for us all... anyway we'll soon know."

But he was wrong about that at least, and it was not until late in the afternoon that we were summonsed back to court with the news that the jury had asked a question of the judge by passing a note to him via the Jury Bailiff, so that we were all required to return to court to listen to his answer.

When the court had re-assembled the judge came in and we all made our bows and listened to the judge say, "Members of the jury, I have been handed this note by your Bailiff in which you ask a question of the court and I am proposing to read your note out to the court. You say, 'We believe that the defendant is in need of medical treatment as recommended by Dr Hambly – but we cannot be sure that the fatal shot was fired on purpose rather than by accident – can the court now make an order that she should receive the recommended medical treatment?'

"Members of the jury. I must ask you, are the contents of this note agreed by you all? In particular that you cannot be sure that the fatal shot was fired on purpose rather than by accident?"

The foreman of the jury was an earnest looking man, who might well have been a solicitor's clerk himself. He now stood to his feet and said, "My Lord, that is the position exactly – we cannot be sure."

"In that case," said the judge, as indeed he had to, whatever his personal views might be, "it means that the prosecution have failed to prove their case and there is only one verdict which you could possibly return and this I now direct you to do, your verdict must be 'not guilty' – Mr Clerk put the question to the jury."

The Clerk of the Court stood up and said the time honoured words, "Members of the jury are you agreed upon your verdict?"

"My Lord we are."

"And do you find the accused, Isabel Mary Earle, guilty or not guilty of the capital murder of Henry John Earle?"

"Not guilty, My Lord."

"And that is the verdict of you all?" asked the clerk as the rules said he had to, and he received, of course, the expected reply.

"It is."

"Then there remains only one order I can make," said Mr Justice Scrutton. "Let her be discharged – I can make no other order, but I do hope that she will be looked after. Officer…" he addressed D.C Trevor Hughes, one of the officers who had given evidence in the case. Detective Chief Inspector Hollingsworth had been called out of court for some urgent business and had left D.C. Hughes in charge in his absence. This same young, rather good-looking, policeman had earlier given evidence that he had been one of the Police Party who had searched 12, Clacton Street unsuccessfully on an occasion a few weeks before the fatal day when he had been suspected of harbouring firearms as part of his nefarious calling as a "Minder", "would you see

that the defendant is taken back to her home? Mrs Collins..."
and Elsie Collins who had remained at he back of the court stood
up looking gratified. "Would you kindly accompany your friend
back home? And Dr Hambly, I see that you are still here as well,
would you very kindly go too, just in case some medical help is
needed? I do not know if it is possible for you to give any
treatment and I understood from your evidence that in any event,
in your opinion Mrs Earle will recover her powers of speech
eventually?"

Mary Hambly rose to her feet.

"Yes, My Lord that is my opinion. In fact now that all the
trauma of her imprisonment and her trial over the past few days
is over, my own opinion is that she might recover her speech
quite soon. I am happy to go with her and do anything I can. I
will certainly look in on her, from time to time, if she is
agreeable."

"Thank you very much. I think that that would be most
helpful and I, at least, would be much happier to think that you
would. Now members of the jury", said the judge, "that
concludes your duties as jurors in what has been a particularly
difficult and stressful case. You are now discharged from further
jury service during these sessions and are free to leave..." And
so they did, glancing curiously at Isabel Earle as she stepped
down from the dock to be greeted by the rather good-looking
young police officer and Elsie Collins.

I looked at the jury as they filed out of their box for the last
time. They had been more that a little concerned I thought, for
that same young figure in the dock, who was now standing in the
well of the court. I looked at her once more to see what effect the
verdict had had upon her. After all it would have been perfectly
open to the jury to have accepted the case for the prosecution as
it had been presented to them and before I had started to do my

humble best to construct some kind of defence for my silent client. They could have rejected everything that the doctors had had to say on both sides. The verdict was entirely up to them. They might have had their own ideas. Isabel Earle had certainly been in danger of death by hanging and I knew that Mervyn Griffiths had thought that this would have been the most probable, as well as the right result. The moment he had heard the verdict from the foreman of the jury, the judge's clerk had moved from his position just behind his judge, where he had been holding the black velvet cushion bearing the dreaded black cap without which no sentence of death could be passed. He had unobtrusively placed it out of sight in a drawer before him. Ready, I thought, for the next case of capital murder waiting to be tried, but no more any kind of threat to Isabel Earle. The judge's chaplain also stood down with palpable relief. It would not be necessary for him to invoke the deity to have mercy on the soul of Isabel Earle that day.

It also meant that I did not have to make any speech in mitigation of sentence. None would have been necessary if Isabel had been found to have been guilty of capital murder without qualification, since only one sentence was possible. But if she had been found to have been guilty of killing her husband with diminished responsibility so that it was only manslaughter, why then I should have had to do my very utmost to get her as short a sentence of imprisonment as possible and my speech was all prepared:

"May it please you M'Lord", I should have began in the time-honoured fashion. "Your Lordship has already heard of the excellent previous conduct of this young defendant. Only twenty two year old when she married the older, more experienced Henry Earle, I accept," I would have said, "as I have to by reason of the jury's verdict, that it was an intentional act on her part which caused his death. I accept that she must have seized the weapon in question. It seems certain that it was already loaded, since no one has suggested that Mrs Earle herself had any knowledge of firearms or of their use or would even have been able to load it herself. The possibility of the death of Henry Earle by accident in a struggle, has been rejected by the jury's verdict of guilty of manslaughter by reason of diminished responsibility, and of course, I must accept that too. But what this means, according to the evidence of Dr Hambly, which the jury clearly preferred to the evidence of the psychiatrists called by the prosecution, is that at the time she did not really know what she was doing. She just cracked. Having lived a life overshadowed by her love for her husband, she suddenly discovered that it had all been a fake on his part – there was no time for her to reflect. No time to calm down. No friend to turn to, for advice. She would have recovered, of course, as Dr Hambly says that now surely she will, under her treatment – but just for that moment she was living out the thoughts expressed by the poet William Congreve more eloquently than I could hope to compete with:

Heaven has no rage, like love to hatred turn'd,
Nor Hell a fury, like a woman scorn'd.

"I accordingly ask your Lordship to say that this is an exceptional case, as indeed I believe it must be, and to allow the defendant to retain her liberty by undergoing a period of probation so that she may receive the guidance of a Probation Officer and receive the medical attention that Dr Hambly has already promised to give her – in the hope, and Dr Hambly's expectation, that before too long she will have recovered her sanity; have got back her powers of speech and taken her place once more among her friends, as a well respected member of the Society of Stoke Newington."

I would have sat down, I had hoped, to a quiet murmur of approval. This was now denied me and the speech I had rehearsed the night before in front of the mirror in my bedroom, would never be made. But of course it was much, much better to achieve such a notable success. And I watched the silent Isabel being taken away between her flanking party. She paused for a moment just before leaving the court and looked directly at me – the man who had, arguably saved her from the gallows. Her right eye again seemed to drop just for a moment – could that be the very faintest suggestion of a wink? The party of her friends in the gallery noisily dispersed to their own homes, and no doubt many a good talk about it all. As I was bundling up my papers Mervyn Griffith came across to me to say:

"Well, young Tam, that was a very good result for you – many would say, including my instructing solicitor, that she should have been hanged for a callous murder – anyway something like 21 months for manslaughter by reason of diminished responsibility would also have been a very lenient sentence – but to have got her off altogether is quite a triumph, even if it does mean that she will remain a considerable danger to the public!"

"Well Mervyn, I agree it could have been horribly worse – although I must say that I always fancied my chances of getting a verdict of 'not guilty' – although I don't believe that the judge was really on my side. The Scrutton sneer was very noticeable. I think he thought like you that she was a bit of a danger. I don't think so. The only possible repetition could be in similar circumstances in my view. And how often are you going to find that young woman in similar circumstances, and with a loaded gun ready to her hand? And confronted by a man who has spurned her? I think myself that she is really quite a beauty – may be very nice, Elsie Collins certainly thought so."

"Well, you certainly won a cause we all thought was lost – and I did think that you did it very well."

And so, with these words of praise ringing in my ears, I went to disrobe and then to make my way back to Chambers at 6, Damson Court. "Another day, another dollar" I thought to myself and began to wonder what fresh delights in the way of the next brief, Challen might have waiting for me. The moment of fame by way of success for Isabel Earle and the resultant publicity, might mean that there would be something of a similar nature waiting for me before too long, although I hardly dared hope for anything quite as exciting.

And so life went on. My friendship with Mary Hambly intensified. We had renewed our friendship by meeting again at the Medico-Legal Society which we had both joined and she was very pleased that I had recommended her for the case, which had intrigued her as much as it had me. It had thrown us together. It was only natural that we should discuss it, and it was no surprise to me when Mary told me that her opinion on the matter had been proved right; that Isabel Earle had fully recovered her powers of speech the very first time she had visited her after the trial. When she had visited her the very next day she found that she could talk again very well. The young police officer in the case had also been there and she had even wondered if there might be a hint of a new romance in the life of Isabel Earle. In the summer Mary and I found ourselves having a brief holiday in Paris. We both wanted to look in at the wonders of the Louvre. Moving from one Old Master painting to the next I was suddenly struck with a sense of déjà vu. Here was someone I actually knew. The same beautiful serene face. The same very faint half smile. The same sense of magic. I hardly needed to read the words on the small brass plate to know that this was that wonderful masterpiece, by Leonardo da Vinci, the Mona Lisa. As I stared at the beautiful face, just for a moment the right eye seemed to drop by a fraction in the form of a wink. I looked again but I could not really be sure. But then I had never been at all sure either, about that faint suggestion of a wink from Isabel Earle in the dock at the Old Bailey. I looked at Mary but she seemed only to be seeing a beautiful painting.

The Law is the true embodiment
Of everything that's excellent.
It has no kind of fault or flaw,
And I, my Lords, embody the Law.

Iolanthe

Chapter Three

It takes quite a time to become a Detective Chief Inspector. But here I was in 1961, George Hollingsworth, stationed at Shoreditch Police Station in Stoke Newington High Street N16, where I had now been for the past two years. To get this far, you have to know the law itself. Of course not like a lawyer, but as a policeman. That is to say you have to have a working knowledge of the criminal law and the practice and procedures of the various criminal courts. It brings you into close contact with the lawyers, and on the whole, I must say, I found them a pretty good class of people. With their own foibles of course, some of them rather snooty, most had been to university and quite a few to Eton or Harrow or somewhere like that. But they usually had a good sense of humour and, particularly if they were appearing for the prosecution, a proper respect for the police, for whom, they were likely to be appearing in most of their cases in the courts.

Of course there would be some of them who did work for defendants as well, but I found that most of the counsel appearing for the police did little other work. To be a good cop, means that you have to keep your own nose clean. But that is not really all that difficult, because if you are any kind of a "good cop" you are basically honest and really do have a good respect for the law itself. And of course, for the magistrates and judges who administer it.

If you are to get on at all in your profession, particularly if you want to become a detective, you must acquire a good knowledge of human nature. Not only that of the normal law-abiding citizen, but also that of that other part of the population, natural enemies of the constabulary – the criminals. About the only generalisation I could give you, after more than 25 years in the force and most of them doing detection work, is that they are as infinitely various as every other section of the community. The only difference being, the lack of honesty, which marks them out from the rest of us; since I believe that the vast majority, including of course most policemen, have never had a really dishonest thought or done a really dishonest thing. From this, being perhaps a little cynical, or maybe just realistic, I exclude the little evasions of failing to return the receipt of too much change on a purchase, or the return for Income Tax of some exceptional gift for "services rendered".

The aspiring detective, and this I certainly was, has to get into the skin of his adversary. He must try to understand the criminal mind. He must try to think what an astute criminal might think and do, in any given set of circumstances. He also gets to learn, sadly, that his own colleagues are not invariably as honest and as upright as they ought to be in every respect. That not all of them, upholders of the law as they are, have never had a dishonest thought or done a dishonest thing. I am not only thinking of those who actually become "bent" and turn to crime themselves. There are only a few but still quite enough of these. I have known apparently upright police officers, who would take part in a raid on suspected premises. It might be to search for the results of a burglary or the haul of a bank robbery. And then, the information which had caused the raid to be made, turning out to be correct, not all of the property recovered would be handed in at the nick. Very difficult for a protesting man accused of being a receiver of stolen property, to declare that he had in fact received more stolen goods than he was actually accused of. That some had "gone missing" and must have been taken by the police themselves. Anyway the missing property would to some extent reduce the value of the goods and the seriousness of the offence with which he was charged. To argue that there had in fact been more, would also amount to an admission that he had received the rest of them, so that he would be guilty of the offence of receiving anyway. Much better for him not to upset the dishonest officers but instead, perhaps to do some kind of deal with them? "If I keep my mouth shut, maybe you could say just 'ow co-operative I was? Keep me out of gaol, guv. I've a clean record and a wife an' kids as well."

Unfortunately there are other possibilities for the dishonest cop to make money on the side. He is in a position of power as far as the arrested criminal is concerned, particularly if he is the officer in charge of the case. A particular example is in the case of the granting or refusal of bail at the Magistrates' Court. Any accused person who has been arrested, must be brought before a court of law at the first possible opportunity. This is an essential part of the law as a protection from any possibility of our becoming a police state. I think it must have been included in "Magna Carta". It means that every arrested person is given the first possible opportunity to make representations to a court which has the power to set him free. Then inevitably comes the question of whether or not bail should be granted, so that he does go free until his case is heard; or whether it is refused in which case he remains in police custody. But bail applications are heard right at the beginning of the day in court and are usually regarded by the magistrates as something of a formality. If the police do not oppose an application for bail then it is always granted, while if they do oppose, then it is generally refused. A contested bail application sometimes means that the defendant has instructed lawyers already, knowing that bail is likely to be opposed, but in many cases, particularly at the first appearance of the accused before a court, they have not been. If no lawyers have been instructed for the defendant, it increases the power of the police, which usually means that of the officer who appears in court, to say one way or the other, "There is no objection to bail or bail is opposed by the police."

There are many legitimate reasons for the police to oppose bail. There is the single compelling reason of "the seriousness of the offence". Those accused of murder were never granted bail. There is the fear expressed by the police, that if granted bail the accused man will commit further offences. There is the fear that if released on bail, the accused man will tamper with the evidence against him by interfering with the witnesses for the prosecution. Telling them in fact, that if they tell the truth, he and his friends will "do them up" – or their mothers or their sisters or their friends. But if the police officer in court only says that bail is not opposed, why then the accused is almost certain to be granted bail and to go free – at least for the moment. This does give the officer in charge of the case a great deal of power. It can be abused.

The most obvious example of this that I ever saw was, once when I was a young policeman, sitting in court waiting for my own case to come on, I listened to another much more serious case, Regina versus John Trafford, which was also in the list for hearing that day. The accused duly appeared in the dock, a decidedly nasty looking bit of work, wearing I happened to notice, a rather fine and spectacular Rolex watch on his wrist. The result I reflected, most probably of some earlier piece of

82

crime. He was accused I heard, of burglary, that serious offence of entering a private dwelling house by night, with the intention of committing theft, therein. It was his first appearance in court on this charge. The police enquiries were not complete said Detective Sergeant Paul Bush, in charge of the case, and there was a formal remand in custody for seven days, no bail being applied for. I was not surprised, since I had been involved with this particular defendant before, and knew that he was only too "well known to the police", likely to re-offend and, for that reason, unlikely to be granted bail. But my own case was remanded for seven days too so that I was in the same court in a week's time when John Trafford next appeared.

"Is there any application for bail?" asked the clerk.

"Yes Sir, I understand that he does want to apply for bail," said D.S. Bush.

"And do the police oppose that?"

"No, Sir."

Well, that was a surprise, to me at least, and judging by the expression on her face to Trafford's wife, as well.

"Then bail is granted if he can find two sureties in the sum of £200 each, to the satisfactory to the police, for his appearance at the committal stage on 23rd March," said the Chairman of the Bench.

The satisfied smile on the face of the defendant seemed to show that he had no fears about finding the sureties.

Young as I was, I knew that in most similar cases there would and should, have been serious opposition to bail, on the grounds that Trafford would commit further offences to add to the string of convictions he already had. It was a few days later that I happened to see Detective Sergeant Bush in the police canteen and was struck by the very fine Rolex watch that he was now wearing on his wrist. It looked strangely familiar. But I was a very junior police officer. There has to be discretion in life for those who were ambitious; anyway there were a number of ways in which that watch – or one very like it – could have got onto the wrist of Detective Sergeant Paul Bush. He might have bought it from Trafford? But at what sort of price? This was going to be one possible crime I was certainly not going to stick my neck out and investigate. So I resisted the impulse to say, "Well, that's a very nice new watch you've got Paul", and got on with other things. But perhaps I was not the only one to have a few suspicions; Bush certainly never made Inspector and I was quite relieved to see that he had been assigned to a desk job soon afterwards.

Another example of police "dishonesty" I came across, and carefully avoided myself, was the use of the "verbal". This is a device well known to everyone in the force for securing a conviction in a doubtful case and, of course, to members of the legal profession as well as the criminal fraternity. The officers assigned to a particular matter might know perfectly well that the man they had arrested was guilty of the offence they had charged him with. But there might be doubt about their ability to prove it, because in spite of their own "certain" knowledge, the evidence needed to be sure of convincing a jury should the matter be disputed, might be thin. Hence the supposed need for the use of the verbal. In reality, of course, if the police are unable to prove their case, using available and admissible evidence, then they should either obtain other legitimate evidence or bring no charges. But unfortunately in my view all too often some over zealous and unscrupulous policeman will try to bridge the gap by using a verbal. The most obvious example is "It's a fair cop guv." It is an expression, well known in the realms of fiction. But it also occurs surprisingly often in reality as well, in the evidence of police officers giving evidence in the cases of those they charge with crime but who deny it all and plead "not guilty" at their trials. If it was really true that these words had been said it could only mean that the criminal in question had been happy to admit his guilt at first, but had later decided to try his luck and go for trial before a jury, and deny it all in the hope of being acquitted.

And of course that does happen too. By 1951, when I first became involved in the case against Isabel Jane Earle the favourite verbal had become "Who's grassed on me?" supposed to have been said, usually when the suspect in question was first arrested. If this had really been said it would have been a great advantage for the police in any case because again it was a hidden admission of guilt. There must be something for the unknown somebody to "grass" about and that could surely only be the offence for which the suspect had just been arrested. But how often was it really said? But my early days in the force showed me that very often it was only a fiction, used to bolster a weak case by just a few unscrupulous colleagues.

Sometimes the use of the fictitious verbal could miscarry, disastrously from the point of view of the prosecution. I remember well the case of Bernard Lawson. He was a young and vicious criminal with a string of convictions involving theft and the use of violence. And then one day there was a robbery right in the middle of my own manor of Stoke Newington. A Securicor delivery van had stopped outside Lloyds Bank to make a routine delivery of cash, when suddenly a large blue Jaguar pulled up in front of it in the middle of the crowded High Street. Three men jumped out, leaving an accomplice sitting at the driving wheel ready to speed away as soon as the robbery was complete. All these men wore black stockings pulled well down over their faces. The three men were armed with black rods which looked like chair-legs but which made frightening cudgels in their hands of those who now waved them in the faces of the frightened Securicor delivery men who had no protection against them. It was not very surprising that two of the bags were seized. One of the guards did resist by trying to throw his bag of bank notes high into the air and into the crowd of passing shoppers. But his bravery was rewarded with a hard blow to his head and he dropped to the ground. The other bags were seized and within a matter of seconds the three men had jumped back into their car which had sped away.

While all of this was happening the startled shoppers had little chance to intervene. Two local shopkeepers promptly dialled 999 and very soon police cars were on the scene. Of course, they were too late; but they did find the car which had been involved. A quick-witted housewife who had even taken down the registration number had accurately described it. And there it was in a back street not very far away. The doors were still open as evidence of recent flight and unsurprisingly there was no sign of the missing bank delivery bags. But there was one of the black chair legs, which had been described as having been used as makeshift cudgels in the robbery. It was of a type which is sold as part of rather cheap chairs which can be taken home in separate pieces and then put together. When forensic experts examined it there was a very clear fingerprint upon it. In no time at all the Finger Print Department at Scotland Yard had identified the owner of it.

Bernard Lawson was well known to us and there was every reason for his fingerprints to be on our files. A man of 28, he already had a long string of convictions which had started when Bernie, at the tender age of eleven, had been convicted of stealing from the handbag of a friend of his mother's who had come into the house to have a cup of tea and a gossip. His "form" included several offences of violence and one previous wages snatch. And now we surely had him by the heels for this latest robbery. But where was he? He was not to be found in any of his usual haunts and it was several weeks before he was arrested. And several weeks more before I found myself looking at the papers in the case, which included of course the depositions, the record of the proceedings in the North London Magistrates' Court which had committed him for trial. I then read of Bernie's arrest. A patrolling police car had spotted him in Hoxton Market not very far from the scene of the crime itself. It was later established that Bernie had spent most of the intervening time in Marbella in sunny Spain and none of the stolen money was ever recovered so that he must have been having a pretty good time with the signorinas.

I was a Detective Sergeant at the time and read the papers in the case to see that P.C. Pryor had called out, "Bernie – come over here, we've been looking for you."

And Bernard Lawson had duly come over to the police car and bent down at the driver's window to say, so the depositions read, without any further prompting, "If it's the blagging in the 'igh Street your after – I don' mind goin' down for the motor – but I never rolled the geezer."

Being translated from the cockney this meant that, "If you want to ask me about the robbery in the High Street, I don't mind admitting that I was the driver but I deny that I ever hit anyone."

And I did not like the sound of it at all. This was an almost copybook verbal. But would the mean mouthed, experienced Bernie that I knew ever have said a word? I doubted it. But there was no way to leave that part of the evidence out at the forthcoming trial at the Old Bailey. And anyway the rest of the evidence looked conclusive. So why had Pc Pryor bothered, if I was right, in adding a quite unnecessary untruth to what was already a convincing case? I wondered and was left pondering upon the fallibility of some police officers who cannot resist embroidering upon an already convincing narrative.

The account in the depositions went on to describe how Bernie had been taken back to Stoke Newington station and questioned by my experienced CID team.

"How do you account for the fact that your fingerprints were found upon the chair leg, in the back of that blue Jaguar car, DHT 189 which was undoubtedly the one used in the raid, Bernie?"

"Well, it's like this guv" – obviously even Bernie realised that he would have to give some explanation for this damning piece of evidence – "a day or two 'afor they done the bank job… from wot I 'eard… I was in Islington 'aving a drink with a mate. When this bloke who was a friend of 'is, come over and joined us, so we all 'ad a drink together. Well it come to near closing time and this other bloke, 'is name was Albert, said wi'out me askin' as 'ow 'e could give me a lift 'ome 'cos it 'ad come out 'e lived rarnd my way. 'Your on mate', I said and 'e did. Well what should I see on the back seat of 'is car but these chair legs. So I just picked one up to see what it was. Out of curiosity like – that's what must 'ave done it."

"So who is your friend Albert and where can we find him?"

"Not a friend so much, just a pal of Bill Gurney who was in the pub that night."

"And where can we find Bill Gurney to corroborate all of this?"

"Well I think 'e might be out in Marbella, but I don' really know."

And indeed Bill Gurney remained out of our clutches until well after Bernie's trial. But what a very inadequate explanation that was, I thought as I looked at the papers. And I had no doubt myself but that Bernie was guilty as charged. But what might a clever counsel make of the verbals? I wondered. And I was soon to find out. Some weeks later I made a point of looking in at Bernie's trial in Court 2 of the Central Criminal Court, the Old Bailey, and I was just in time to hear the final speech of Tam Pearse, the young counsel instructed on behalf of Bernie, who was already making a name for himself; so much so that it was already being said that no case was completely hopeless if a defendant had Tam Pearse on his side. I listened with respect as I heard him saying:

"...well, members of the jury, we've heard all about the evidence of the robbery in the High Street and that some things looking like chair legs something like Exhibit 1 in this case, had been used. We've heard all about the interviews that the officers had with my client Mr Bernard Lawson, and it may be, I can't say, that there were some grounds for suspicion of Mr Lawson by the police. But you will hear from My Lord, the learned judge when he comes to make his summing up of the case to you, that mere suspicion is not enough. You must be sure that the defendant is guilty before you bring in a verdict of guilty. And how can you possibly be sure when you look at the whole of the evidence in this case as M'Lud the learned judge is bound to tell you that you must? That evidence includes the evidence of two police officers that they stopped Mr Lawson in Hoxton Market, a good many weeks later and called him to their car. He bent down and said at once, without any prompting:

"'...if it's the blagging in the 'igh street, you mean, I don't mind going down fer the mo'er but I never rolled the geezer...'

"Well, you've seen Mr Lawson in Court. You've heard him give evidence. You may think that he is probably a man of few words, it is entirely a matter for you to say, but you may think that he would not be very good at explaining himself in a difficult situation. But can you possibly believe that he would virtually admit being a party to this serious offence, because serious it undoubtedly is. Unprompted. Unasked. Without any Caution having been previously given, by saying"... and Tam Pearse's voice rose to a high pitch of complete incredulity as he repeated the words, with a very fair imitation of Bernie's cockney accent:

"'...if it's the blagging in the 'igh Street, you mean, I don't mind going darn fer the mo'er but I never rolled the geezer.'

"You see, members of the jury, it has been known for police officers to put words into the mouths of defendants as a seeming admission of their guilt. It is called verbaling them. Now if you simply cannot credit that the defendant ever said anything of the sort; why then you could not be sure of any of it could you? You would have no choice, no option at all, you could not accept part of their case and reject the rest. You will have to acquit."

Tam Pearse sat down and the jury sat back in their seats and listened patiently while the judge, the Recorder of London,

Eustace Beesley, went through it all. But he said, as I knew that he was bound to, that whether the jury believed the evidence, or any part of it, was their function alone and not his as they were the sole judges of fact. And so it came as no surprise to me to hear the jury, after a very short period of deliberation, return to court and bring in a verdict of "not guilty". And so I went back to Stoke Newington police station. At an early opportunity I let it be known how displeased I was at the outcome of the case of Regina versus Bernard Lawson. I made it quite clear that an obviously guilty man had escaped his just reward, solely because of the use of the untrue verbal. I made it plain that it must not happen again. Certainly not when we had a very good case without it – but of course, it must not happen at all, even when we had not. My officers must be as honest as anyone possibly could be.

There could be no question of anybody planting any fictitious admission into the mouth of the fair Isabel Earle I thought, as I looked at her in the mean little hallway of 12 Clacton Street, just off Stoke Newington High Street. She was just standing there against the wall of her own house, looking strangely calm and detached and not saying a word. It was mid-afternoon and I had been on duty in my office in Shoreditch Police Station, when the call first came through. There had been a shooting, perhaps some kind of domestic drama between husband and wife, but a man lay dead in the street outside his own house. It seemed that it was Henry Earle its owner, and it looked as if he had been shot dead by his wife, the only other person present when it all happened. And Henry Earle was a name I knew. In fact it was known very well to most of the officers at Shoreditch Police Station. He was a "Minder" and like most others carrying out this lucrative trade in the criminal

91

fraternity of North and East London at that time, he was on the record at least a "man of good character". He was too fly by half to have been caught out.

I remembered the occasion some few weeks before when I had ordered the raid, my men had been armed with a search warrant granted by magistrates on the basis of "information received". Although our information was thought to be very reliable, to my considerable disappointment a very thorough search had found nothing in the nature of a deadly weapon, or for that matter anything in the way of stolen property either. So Earle continued his life at liberty, and the police, and me in particular, were left fuming at the unreliability of some police informers. We had tried to catch Henry Earle in possession of the weapons we believed that he harboured. But we had failed; now it looked as if we never should catch him at anything and the poor frail-looking young woman, standing in the hall leaning against the wall was a widow by her own act – or that is what it certainly looked like. She had apparently been wounded herself in whatever fracas had occurred that day. An ambulance man had dressed the flesh wound to her thigh and I was told that it gave no cause for alarm but was likely to be painful. The "Scene of Crime Squad" from my own station was already hard at work when I had arrived. There were five of them, including a finger-print expert, a firearms specialist and, of course, the obligatory WPC who was standing beside Isabel Earle apparently trying to comfort her. She would be careful not to start the important task of asking her, "What the hell happened then?" since that would be up to me. Mrs Earle herself was silent and seemed to be emotionless, quite withdrawn; as well she might be I thought, having just killed her husband. I told WPC Claire Davies to take her into her own sitting room, to sit her down and I would get someone to make them both tea; and to ask her no questions but of course to note down anything at all that she might happen to blurt out. I wanted first of all to have a good look at the body of Henry Earle lying still on the pavement outside. Three other officers were already starting the house-to-house enquiries. I was pleased to see that young D.C. Trevor Hughes was standing beside me. He had been involved in the search of the house not very long before, and since he would remember something of the lay out, I asked him to search it again. I knew that he was meant to be off-duty so it was good to see such keenness in the good-looking young man who had recently been transferred to Shoreditch C.I.D. from the uniformed branch, as a recognition of his keenness and ability.

The group round the prostrate figure on the pavement parted at my approach, and there he lay. More dignified in death than Henry Earle had ever been in life. Lying on his face with his right arm outstretched and just beyond it an old-fashioned but deadly Colt .45 revolver. It had been carefully taken up already by an officer who had obeyed the rules carefully, making sure that he did not disturb the fingerprints upon it before examining it to ensure that it was no longer a danger to the public, and then replacing it exactly where it had been to be examined in detail by the fingerprint expert who was waiting nearby. There was a large pool of blood round the head of the dead man. There was other blood on the pavement in patches near his body. And there was a trail of blood leading back to the door of the house. An ambulance had arrived and a doctor from a nearby medical surgery, had already examined the body of Henry Earle and pronounced the obvious, that his life was extinct. The ambulance would take him only to the morgue and the detailed examination of the pathologist, but I noticed that there seemed to be signs of other bullet wounds besides the one which had killed him; I thought that this must surely have been the one to his head.

The crowd of interested passers-by and neighbours, was now being controlled by some officers of the uniformed branch and I saw with satisfaction that enquiries of the neighbours by house to house visits was already under way. So I could turn my attention to the real business in hand and went with Detective Sergeant Bill Hollings back to the house to try to unravel the events of that day. I called WPC Davies out of the sitting room, leaving Isabel Earle in the temporary charge of a uniformed officer.

"What has she said?" I asked with interest.

"She hasn't said a word."

"Nothing at all? No kind of explanation? No kind of enquiry even as to whether her husband is dead or not?"

"She has not said a single thing… she didn't even thank me when I gave her a cup of tea… she hasn't even drunk it, just put it down. I have not cautioned her yet, I felt I should leave that to you, Sir."

Well that was something which should be done at once. I knew that there was nobody else in the house. A man lay dead outside. I knew from the very first reports that a number of shots had been heard before Henry Earle had burst out of the house, and that Isabel Earle had been shot through the leg. The only possibilities seemed to be that she had shot him and then herself. It seemed to be out of the question that he had committed suicide. Perhaps for reasons unknown, husband and wife had fallen out bitterly and violently. Lethal weapons were readily to hand in that house as we had long suspected, in spite of our recent fruitless search for them. So there must have been some kind of furious quarrel involving the loaded revolver, now safely in the custody of the forensic experts in my squad. As the only person who could possibly have been involved apart from the dead man, Isabel Earle must be guilty of the murder or at least of the manslaughter, of her husband. So she had to be cautioned before being arrested and taken down to Shoreditch Police Station.

We went into the room where Mrs Earle stood awaiting us with a completely blank expression upon her face. I noticed that she was wearing a quiet, grey dress which seemed to fit the quiet, sort of person that she seemed to be, although I knew that it was of the style just become fashionable. It was the "new-look" stretching to below the knees. In the wartime years not long since, all materials were in such short supply that the shortage had itself dictated fashion, so that skirts did not extend below a woman's knees. It was a little debatable as to whether this was a change for the better, but at least it seemed that Isabel had bought herself a new dress fairly recently. Undoubtedly she was very attractive, her long dark hair hanging down behind her tied by a dark blue ribbon which must, surely, be made of silk. I noted that Detective Sergeant Hollings was standing beside me with his notebook at the ready and his pencil poised.

"Isabel Earle, is that your name?" I asked and she made no reply, but of course I knew who she was. And so I continued, "I am arresting you on suspicion of the murder of Henry Earle, your husband, by shooting him… You need say nothing…. but I must warn you that anything that you do say, will be taken down in writing and may be used in evidence at your trial."

She said not a word but continued to look at me silently with a faintly puzzled expression upon her face. As if to say, "well it is all very strange, but I couldn't possibly say what all this is about, or what you are all doing here in my home?" So she was led away still in silence, and I began my own examination of the house which was already being searched thoroughly by my scene of crime team. I noticed with interest that they had already uncovered a pile of assorted weapons, none of which had been there at the time of the earlier search. So our suspicions had been right, and there must have been some kind of tip-off, and everything of an incriminating nature must have been spirited away until our search had finished and they could safely be returned. What did this mean I wondered? Perhaps there was some bent copper in my own station, who had tipped the wink to Henry Earle in exchange for a heavy bribe? But I did not think so. Or could it have been that the wily Henry Earle himself, knowing that he was under suspicion, had caused word to be passed to some police informer, so that his own house was raided, but at a time when he had been careful to see that there was nothing there for us to find? Or, had the Informer, or indeed just possibly, someone else at Stoke Newington been guilty of some double dealing? I resolved to explore these possibilities as soon as I could, since the idea of having a traitor in the camp was too terrible to contemplate.

I knew that the Colt .45 could contain only six rounds and it appeared that it had been fully loaded. A preliminary examination of the body had shown that there had been two other flesh wounds neither serious. Only one bullet remained in Earle's body which was the one which had killed him and which must have remained in his head, since there was no exit wound visible. Five more bullets of .45 calibre had been found in the house, distorted in various ways by the effect of impact upon parts of a human body, or the walls of the house. In each case the bullet was now encased in a plastic bag and carefully numbered. It was difficult to tell whether any of these bore traces of human blood, either that of Earle or of Isabel, but subsequent tests would reveal the truth and then we should know approximately where each shot had been fired as well as exactly where each had ended up, since the numbers on the plastic bags corresponded with chalk marks on different places scattered round the house and carefully photographed. The numbers of course were arbitrary and corresponded with the order in which D.S. Hollings, leading the search, had found them, which might or might not have been the order in which they had been fired. There was a patch of blood on the hall floor close to the bullet numbered "3" and my guess, subsequently confirmed by forensic tests, was that this must have been the one which had caused Isabel Earle's own injury. Then there were the two further bullets found also in the hall and the fatal wound, with numbers 1 and 2 found in the kitchen. It did rather look as if the firing had started in the kitchen, progressed into the hall, and that the last shot had been fired as the wretched Henry Earle struggled to escape, and perhaps had managed to get the door open – but too late. The last shot being fired probably while he was actually at the half opened door. At least this was a reasonable working hypothesis to begin with until we knew exactly, from the forensic examination of the spent bullets.

I went into the kitchen, where perhaps it had all started. Here the two bullets found had been in the wall and the ceiling, both close to an old-fashioned iron kitchen range. So far everything fitted but I did notice that on the front of the kitchen range there was a splash of bright metal which could well have been caused by a bullet fired at fairly close range. But if so where was that bullet? It could certainly have been one of those in the wall or kitchen nearby although neither of these, as I examined them in their individual plastic bags, seemed to be as distorted as I would have expected, if it had caused the bright splash of colour on the front of the black iron cooker. But of course I might be wrong, since bullets behaved in funny ways when hitting solid objects like a solid iron cooker. One might have caused the obvious mark but ricocheted off still unaltered in shape itself. Or, of course, the mark might have been caused at a slightly earlier time in any one of a thousand ways, and not by a bullet at all but by a hard blow from almost anything else that was metallic. I gave the necessary instructions that the house should be boarded up so that it was preserved for later more thorough forensic examination, and so that the curious residents of Clacton Street should be kept at bay. Enquiries of them were still going on, although I suspected that there was very little that any of them could say which would amount to worthwhile evidence to go before a court of law. It was an exercise that had to be gone through although it seemed more likely they would only obtain tittle-tattle and local gossip about a household which must have been a strange one, even by the standards of Shoreditch, but local gossip could still be useful.

Before leaving the scene and making for my own office at Shoreditch nick I had a brief word with my officers who had been talking to the neighbours and gathered them about me.

"So what have you come up with as to the background?" I asked.

Richard Prendergast was a fatherly figure at Shoreditch, the sort of officer who was the salt of the earth and, unlikely to get much further than the Sergeant he was, kindly and inspiring confidence. Just the right man to talk to the housewives of Stoke Newington to gain their confidence and make them feel at ease.

"Well, Sir, I've been talking to a Mrs Elsie Collins from Number 14, next door. She's a good friend of Isabel Earle, she says, and knew her husband Henry as well. Apparently Mrs Collins knows all about Henry's dubious reputation with guns and consorting with criminals. She also says that he did not treat

Isabel at all well and was always knocking her about. But her friend was in love with her husband in spite of everything. Until he started to go about with another woman. Irene Barret the wife of John Barret. We know all about John Barret, Sir, of course. At the moment he is doing a long stretch for burglary so he is inside in Wandsworth and out of the way. But he could well have had dealings with Earle in the past. Anyway the gossip is that Henry Earle took up with Irene, knowing her husband was out of the way and it all became a very big deal for them. He was all set to go off with her and leave Isabel. And, Mrs Collins says, the rumour was that Henry had boasted about it and was going to tell Isabel he was going to leave her this very day. So it just could be that that, was what triggered the whole thing off. Mrs Collins seems quite sure of it."

"But if he was knocking her about surely she would be rather glad to be rid of him?" I objected.

"Well, women are funny creatures, Sir, you might think that; and for that matter so might I – you'd think that she would be well rid of him. She's a pretty enough young women too and I'd be surprised if she couldn't find someone else quite soon. Someone who might suit her a lot better. But as I say Sir, women are funny creatures…" He must have caught sight of my amused look and continued, "…with all respect to Mrs Hollingsworth, and of course there are many notable exceptions, but anyway some women are funny creatures and Elsie Collins seems to think that that was the cause of it all."

Well I'd heard of stranger things. I thought of Isabel Earle standing mute and puzzled in the hallway of her house. She was certainly pretty, although beautiful might have been a better word to describe her. Not a word that would apply to many on my beat in North London but it did seem to fit her. There was something about her immobile face and slightly puzzled look that reminded of some great painting of the past I had once seen and for some reason remembered. She was certainly much too good for the very nasty young criminal who she had married. But it doesn't pay to be too much of a philosopher if one is a police officer doing a job, and hoping to get to the very top of a strenuous and demanding profession. It was all very strange but what other reason was there for the awful events of that morning? Shakespeare had once said I seemed to remember, that "Rumour is oft a lying jade" but he had never suggested that that was invariably the case. What was quite certain was that jealousy was no excuse for murder. And a very brutal murder at that. In France perhaps; as a crime passionnel I believed they called it. We had all wondered at it after a lecture at the Staff College in Hendon. There it might have amounted to a defence but certainly not in Shoreditch, I mused as I made my way back to my office and the intensifying difficulties of this strange case.

Some time later I entered the interview room at Shoreditch Police Station with Detective Sergeant Bill Hollings, having had a quiet word with him and an update on the position. We saw that WPC Davies and Isabel Earle were sitting patiently waiting for us and we took our seats behind the desk. I called in the station's shorthand-writer. She was very good at the job and had once been an official shorthand writer at the Middlesex Sessions, so that she certainly knew her stuff, and I should not have to wait continually for her to catch up with my forthcoming dialogue with Isabel.

"I must remind you that you have already been cautioned that you need say nothing; but that anything that you do say will be taken down in writing and may be given in evidence at any subsequent court proceedings there may be... now why don't you take your time, and tell me all about it? In your own words, at your own speed?"

But I need not have bothered to get a shorthand writer of excellent attainments. Isabel Earle said nothing. She just sat in her chair with the same bland look upon her face. Calm, with nothing on her mind, but now perhaps showing hints of a faint surprise – as if she still had no real idea as to why she was there but hoped that before very long we would get her get back to her own home. The only difference was that she was now holding a handbag that I assumed WPC Davies had found for her before leaving home; but she still said not a word.

"Well, as I have explained, it is your right to say nothing at all…" I couldn't help feeling a little rattled myself now. They always said something… even if it was, "I'm not saying nothing guv." But not Isabel Earle… "You can perhaps, do yourself a lot of good, by telling us what happened? If you can give no explanation at all – well you know that your husband is dead – although we are still awaiting the results of a post-mortem examination it seems pretty clear that he died from gun-shot wounds, and probably the one to his head – and there was only one gun, a .45 Colt revolver that seems to have been used. And, for that matter I believe that it must be the one which caused your own injury. You can surely give us some explanation? Would you like to have the help of a lawyer? If you would I could get you one very soon and at no cost to you, to act on your behalf and to advise you in this situation?"

But she still said nothing.

"You see, Mrs Earle," I persisted, "if there is no explanation and there was nobody else in the house, which seems to be the case, why then I must be driven to the conclusion that it was you who fired all those shots, one of which caused the death of your husband. And if it was, and there is no explanation at all from you, why then it looks very much as if it was a deliberate act on your part? Only you can tell me that

101

it was not? That it was all an accident or a mistake – or even that you were provoked to do it? Please say something – please tell me what on earth it was all about?" This was probably going too far but what was I to do? The words of the caution had to be observed and they included the clear statement that she need say nothing. But however bad the appearances might be I wanted to give her every chance before charging her with the wilful murder of her husband, so I adjourned the interview and telephoned the solicitors on duty that day, who happened to be Messrs Purvis and Jarrold a respectable firm in practice close to the Shoreditch Police Station itself. I spoke to Jim Hawkins the Litigation Clerk of the firm and briefly explained the circumstances, and in a very short time Jim Hawkins duly appeared at the door of my office accompanied by his Senior Partner, Richard Purvis himself. Clearly the possibility of an attractive young woman charged with the capital murder of her husband, with all the drama, and no doubt publicity, that might be involved, was enough to attract the presence of the great man himself.

And so I quickly gave them the bare details of the events of that morning. Ushered them into the interview room and arranged for Isabel and her attendant WPC Davies to join them there, before discretely withdrawing to leave them to make what they could of their new client. I had already telephoned Dr Dromgoole, the splendid Irish doctor who happened to be on duty that day as police surgeon, and now he came in to my office where, again, I gave a quick resume of the facts most of which he already knew, and asked him to examine the lady whose husband he had recently pronounced as dead, with a view to deciding what I was possibly going to do with her. She would have to appear before a Magistrates' Court as soon as possible and at most within three days. But there was a lot to be done before then. The good doctor and I went off to the interview room, and as we entered we saw as I had rather expected, two rather puzzled solicitors, a still silent Isabel Earle, and a patient WPC Davies.

"Our client has not said a word," said Mr Purvis. "Not one single word." Not unnaturally he looked a bit upset. "It is quite outside anything I've met with before, after nearly forty years of experience in the courts. Usually they've got far too much to say, although just sometimes they need a bit of skilled coaxing – but this one won't say a single thing."

"I am afraid that we've found that too – it must be something beyond all our experiences and that means that we need a medical opinion, so I have just brought Dr Dromgoole here, who I'm sure you know already, to give her a brief examination. If you gentlemen have quite finished with her for the moment, he might take her into the inner room with WPC Davies to do that, while we stay here. There are quite a few members of the press anxious to talk to us all about the murder – well let's call it that for the moment. If you are agreeable, we might have a brief word with them?"

And so Isabel Earle was ushered out for her medical examination and some eight or nine reporters were ushered into my office. Of course they were full of questions and I explained briefly the essential facts as we knew them. I said nothing about Henry Earle's past history as a Minder. Or the raid that we had carried out on his house such a short while ago. He had had no official criminal record. That was one of the main requirements for his very dubious occupation. So officially "nothing was known against him". I had little doubt however that the ferrets of Fleet Street would find out soon enough what his occupation had been; probably by questioning the neighbours, if not my own men. The bare facts, as I was able to outline them, were stark but dramatic enough to kindle some keen interest from the press. When asked for details I could provide very few. I did just mention that I had heard from some of the neighbours that there could have been family reasons for a sudden furious row between husband and wife, but explained that of course, the police did not go in for gossip. There was no certain way that it could be given in evidence, on oath and before a court of law, I explained. There were enough clues for the press to go on and I knew that before long they would want to be asking the same questions of Mrs Collins as we had, so I reminded them that as a potential witness for the crown they should not speak to her at all.

No sooner had the last of the reporters made a hurried exit to dash back to his office with his "copy", than a flustered looking Dr Dromgoole came back in, to say that he too had been able to make nothing of the lady he had been asked to examine. From the general description of what had apparently happened inside 12, Clacton Street he thought that his patient must be insane but that must be a question for the experts to decide. He looked as puzzled as he sounded and under stress the faint Irish accent that he had, became more pronounced.

"To be honest with ye I never came across the like of it 'afore. She won't say a word to me any more than she has to you, although I explained that it was the doctor/patient relationship that we had, and everything would be in confidence, but it did no good at all, at all. I'll have to call in an expert in Forensic Psychiatry, and I think I must consult with the Home Office as to who that would be – but I know that you'll be wanting to know if she is fit to be charged. I know ye have to bring her before the magistrates and all I can say is that she is quite fit physically. There's no evidence of drink at all. But whether she'll understand a word you are saying is another matter altogether." And with that he bustled out to make his own arrangements for a psychiatrist to examine her.

Richard Purvis and Jim Hawkins had been listening to all that was being said but now departed looking as puzzled as we all felt. Richard Purvis saying as he left, "I'll need to try to get the Legal Aid people to stretch it a bit and allow me to have her examined by a woman psychiatrist I have in mind. If even the police surgeon is in doubt then perhaps the psychiatrists will be as well and I'm beginning to think that it may all turn on the medical opinion on the lady."

So that was that for the moment; I had three days before the end of which under the rules, Isabel would have to be brought before magistrates. By that time I should have had to charge her with some offence or let her go. There was no question that I could possibly do anything but charge the lady with something. She was clearly a grave danger to the public. And murder with the use of a firearm meant – I had a quick look at my text books to remind myself – that under the provisions of the Homicide Act 1957 section 5 (b) it was capital murder, still punishable with the obligatory sentence of death by hanging which the Law still allowed at that time. I had little doubt myself that the half-way house to abolition of the death penalty provided for by the recent Act, would soon be followed by total abolition. For my own part I was all in favour of the death sentence as being appropriate for some cases of murder. The really bad ones, or multiple murders perhaps. But not for all. I grudgingly agreed that the French system of the crime passionel had a lot to recommend it, allowing escape from anything like a sentence of death, for at least some such crimes in exceptional circumstances. To do away with the death penalty altogether would mean the loss of a very serious deterrent from all crimes of violence since any use of lethal weapons must put the criminal in fear for his own life. In any event would it really be so very much better, I asked myself, to substitute life imprisonment, or even a very long sentence? For many the idea of a life behind bars would be more intolerable than the short sharp ending of a broken neck at the end of a noose. You could say that for that reason life imprisonment was the better deterrent. But on the whole I did not agree. Surely that was to maintain a form of barbarism, which could be justified if at all, only by "The Public Good" and could you have anything which was for the public good but which amounted to a very expensive form of barbarism? My ability to speak a little French had been gained after an attachment to the Paris Surete and I knew that I must be careful not to become regarded in the force as anything like an intellectual. Philosophy was clearly out for me, and I must just get on with the job of what to do with Isabel Earle.

There seemed to be no real doubt that she had fired the gun in question and that a shot from it had killed him. An early pathologist's report showed that the bullet to his brain must have caused his almost instantaneous death and only Isabel could have fired it since suicide was certainly not a possibility and there had been no one else there. Regrettable as it was to think of that attractive young woman being hung, it was not after all for me to decide. The doctors would be making their reports very shortly and I was expecting to receive at least a preliminary opinion from Dr Dromgoole's nominee by the end of the next day. That meant that there would have to be a special sitting of the North London Magistrates' Court on Saturday. Holloway Prison in Parkhurst Road was not far away and had good facilities for prisoners on remand and overnight custody, so I arranged for WPC Davies to take her there, and called in young DC Trevor Hughes to tell me what if anything, his search of the house had revealed which might be helpful.

He was a good looking young man and seemed to be just a little bit flustered which I put down to the natural reaction of a young man, in the presence of his boss.

"Well, Trevor what did you find?" I asked.

"Nothing at all out of the ordinary Sir, apart from the large assortment of armoury you will have heard about already – you will probably have heard that the neighbours say that Henry Earle was carrying on with the wife of our old friend John Barret, now doing seven years for robbery with violence. The neighbours seem to think that he might just have told her that he was walking out on her in favour of Irene Barret – that might account for it all."

"Did you think of looking to see if there were any letters – or anything else for that matter, which might substantiate the idea?"

"Well, I did have that thought, Sir as a matter of fact, and I did have a general look round with that in view. I looked in all the drawers, of course. But there was nothing at all that seemed out of the ordinary – except for £250 in old one pound notes stuffed away underneath a floorboard with a German Luger Automatic and that, of course has all been handed in to DS Hollings."

A long training in interviewing every type of miscreant has left me with a sort of sixth sense as to when a witness is in any way uneasy. And for just a moment that sort of sensation flicked across my mind now. But of course that was absurd.

"Well, I do just want to say that it was very keen of you to come along so soon. I know you were off-duty, I believe that you were one of the first to get there and I shall keep it in mind; well done."

"Well, I just happened to be shopping in the High Street near-by on my way home, when I heard the general call on my radio, so of course I came along straight away, Sir."

And out he went leaving me to make the arrangements for Mrs Earle to be taken to Holloway for overnight custody; and then to gather in the reports of the other officers principally involved and to make out my own report and then to go off home, very late for supper to be greeted by my own long suffering wife, who was all too used to putting mine in the oven to be eaten well after she had had her own. The next day I was able to read with interest the preliminary medical opinion of a Dr Harold Rathbone a Consultant Psychiatrist. He knew the facts as reported to him and had examined the patient. Physically she seemed in good health but, like everyone else he had failed to get her to say a word. He was puzzled as to whether this was from sheer lack of co-operation from someone who had just committed a brutal murder or from a total loss of the power of speech. But he had never come across the latter; he felt little doubt that either she could have co-operated, but refused to, or that she could not co-operate because she was as mad as a hatter, "criminally insane". He was more familiar with the McNaughton Rules than I was myself.

To escape the consequences of the usual inevitable sentence of death by hanging for capital murder, it was necessary that the jury should be convinced that the accused person, otherwise guilty of the offence, had either been so insane that she did not know what she was doing – or at least did not know that it was wrong. What did that last bit really mean? I pondered. Would it do if she thought that she was justified by his appalling behaviour? First being violent to her and then, in spite of her own uncomplaining love, going off with another woman? I felt pretty sure that moral justification would never be enough. After

108

all we were not living in France and any test must be applicable to the facts of every case as our own law stood in 1961. So I had very few doubts as to what the outcome would be. She would be found "guilty of capital murder but insane". At least that would mean that the public would be put out of danger that there would be any repetition.

The weeks passed and other cases and other duties claimed my attention until the day of the trial itself. I had however kept up with progress on the case. I had noted the view of Dr Mary Hambly, the psychiatrist called in by the defence. It seemed rather fanciful to me since although I could accept the part about her having been struck dumb, after all I had seen the lady myself, I very much doubted that she could ever return to complete normality as Dr Hambly believed. Isabel was the only one who could have fired all those shots. She was surely guilty. She should be put away. When the trial started before Mr Justice Scrutton at the Old Bailey I was in Court One sitting in front of counsel for the prosecution and beside the solicitor from the Director of Public Prosecutions. I listened to it all intently. My job now, of course, was to see if there was anything at all I could do to help with the prosecution case. Any unexpected developments that might be thrown up by the defence. Any particular danger areas. It was all part of the system that the defence could literally keep their mouths shut as to what their defence was going to be. They did not have to say in advance.

This all stemmed from the days when the defence had no right to give evidence at all. Almost unbelievably by the notions and standards of today, it was only in 1898 that any defendant was allowed to give evidence on his or her own behalf because of the passing of the Revolutionary Criminal Evidence Act in that year. Until then it was for the prosecution to prove their case

109

if they could and not for the defendant to disprove it. The reason for this misguided as it was, was that defendants of the past, were often illiterate and unable to present a case for themselves. Long before the time of Legal Aid or the Poor Prisoners' Defence Certificate, it was almost unheard of that they should be able to provide the money for any advocate to do this on their behalf. So it was generally accepted that it was much fairer for them, that they should have no ability to give evidence at all. Let the prosecution prove the case against them if it could. It seems difficult to believe today but all those thousands of petty thieves who were deported to the penal colonies in Australia and elsewhere, never had the opportunity to say a word in their own defence. Provided always, of course, that the prosecution had been able to prove the case against them to the satisfaction of the jury. That is why there were so many acquittals. Juries were sympathetic to some defendants, then as now, particularly when hanging was the usual sentence for any serious theft. Neither was the thought that it was unfair to allow defendants to speak on their own behalf entirely misplaced. And it was thought to be doing a kindness to the defendant that he could not give evidence and so be subject to ruthless cross-examination by counsel for the prosecution.

The defence knew very well what the case against them was. It was all set out very fully in the depositions, the notes of all the evidence, already given against the defendant at the earlier hearing in the Magistrates' Court which was likely to include, as in the present case, only the police evidence, quite sufficient on its own, to obtain a committal for trial on the charge of capital murder. No medical evidence had been called before the magistrates. This was all left for decision at the trial itself. So that the defence had the added advantage of knowing what was going to happen while the prosecution did not and at the trial itself it would only be possible for the prosecution to call such evidence if they wished to in order to contradict, medical evidence that the defence had first called, to found perhaps, a suggestion of diminished responsibility. They might on the other hand very well decide to just wait and see if the prosecution could prove its case and call no medical evidence so that the prosecution would be powerless to do so either. After all there had been no witnesses to the events themselves. So could it really be proved that Isabel had been a murderess? It was all a matter of inference – but could there be any other inference except that she had fired all those shots with the clear intention of killing her husband?

I listened to the evidence and I heard that clever young barrister Tam Pearse, who had been briefed for the defence, start to cast some doubt on the matter, with his suggestion that it could all have been an accident. The bullet through Isabel's thigh and the fact that the Colt .45 in question had been found close to the dead man's hand, being the foundation for his theory that it might not have been an intentional act at all, but only the result of an accidental firing of the gun during the course of a struggle for possession of it. Mrs Elsie Collins, anxious to help her friend no doubt, gave some support for this idea, and I wondered if the prosecution had been wise to call her as a witness at all, but of course her evidence of the fact that Henry Earle was going to tell Isabel that he was going to leave her, the very day it all happened, did provide a very strong motive for the murder. But for the first time I began to feel some doubts myself. It would be interesting to see if Tam Pearse was prepared to risk everything and call no medical evidence, on the basis that if the jury believed that this theory could not be discounted, then it meant that the prosecution had not made out its case. With the result that Isabel Earle would walk free – with all the dangers that that would involve. I had seen the report of Dr Hambly, which had been made available to the prosecution. I knew that what she said in it, might give the defence a reasonable chance of setting up a defence of diminished responsibility, which would reduce the crime to one of manslaughter only. This would mean that Isabel certainly would not hang and in all probability would receive only a short sentence of imprisonment, or quite likely would escape prison altogether and be put on probation. If Tam Pearse did not call her to give evidence and the jury did not accept the theory that it could all have been an accident, then it meant that that attractive, wan, distant-looking young woman, sitting in the dock would surely hang. I thought that it was not the sort of decision I should like to have to make myself.

And then the die was cast. Tam Pearse called Dr Hambly and we embarked upon the evidence of the eminent doctors called for both sides with their widely different views as to the cause of it all. Once more I reflected on the fact I found increasingly amazing, that highly qualified experts called as witnesses in a court of law, could take such widely different views of the same set of circumstances and, in this case the mental state of a patient. Was it really possible that Isabel was insane and had been at the time of the crime? As our own medical team were asserting with all that certainty that one expects of expert witnesses. I had my own doubts about it as I searched that pale face in the dock for any sign of emotion, and searched in vain. Then there followed counsels' closing speeches and I had to admit that Tam Pearse put the case for an accidental firing of the fatal bullet, in the course of a struggle with clarity and force. But then there followed the summing up of Mr Justice Scrutton. A very sound judge, I thought as I listened to it. He emphasised the danger that the defendant had been that night, the danger that she still remained to us all. He seemed to prefer the view of the prosecution doctors to that of Dr Hambly, but said that after all it was the jury's opinion that counted and not his own. He glossed over the possibility of accident, and few in court could have been in any doubt that he himself thought that it was fanciful. Did he go a bit too far on that point I wondered? I knew that jurors could, as indeed they always should, be independent and that too much persuasion from the Bench had been known to have the opposite effect from that intended.

And then the jury went out to deliberate in their room; and the rest of us all waited or went for coffee, or talked to our friends. I noticed young Trevor Hughes come into court. He brought me a message from Shoreditch that I should get back as soon as possible as there had been a robbery, this time at the Stoke Newington branch of the Trustee Savings Bank and since he was there, and the case might end at any minute, I asked him to take my place. But before I could hurry back to Stoke Newington, there was renewed interest as the Jury Bailiff came in to say that the jury had reached its verdict. Everyone went back to their proper places in court and we all rose as the judge made his entrance, accompanied of course, by his clerk, with the black cap hanging unobtrusively from his hand, and by his chaplain. Then, after the usual courteous bows to and from the Bench, and counsel, and we lesser mortals in the body of the court, we all resumed our seats. I watched the faces of the jurors as they came back into court with the defendant sitting motionless in the dock. Each one as he or she came into the jury box turned to look at Isabel Earle, before taking their seat. It was a sign that I had always thought to be almost infallible, that there was going to be an acquittal. If the jurors were going to convict a young woman of murder, they were human enough not to want to catch her eye. So I was not too surprised to hear them ask the question which, inevitably meant that they had not been convinced that the charge of capital murder had been made out. I waited only to hear the judge discharge the defendant as he had no option but to do. I heard him ask Dr Hambly and Mrs Collins to accompany her to her home. It seemed a bit imprudent to me; after all, two highly qualified doctors had just certified the young woman insane. And so before hurrying back to Shoreditch I asked Trevor Hughes just to see that the group returned to 12, Clacton Street in safety. Well "you can't win them all" I mused on my way back to Stoke Newington. But there remained some questions unanswered and surely Isabel still remained a possible danger to the public, so I resolved to ask DC Hughes just to keep an eye on 12 Clacton Street. After all, his quarters were not far distant. When I did so he agreed with alacrity, confirming my belief that he was going to make a very good detective.

The case remained forcefully in my mind. Were the jury right after all? Had I been wrong throughout? It was certainly a possibility that there had been a struggle for the gun and that Isabel had been wounded during it. If there had been a struggle, then certainly it was conceivable that Henry Earle had received the fatal wound at that same time. It could be argued that the prosecution had not excluded that possibility. But how could they have, when there were no witnesses? So it was all a question of inference. For myself, I was not convinced of the accident theory. It seemed odd to me that Henry Earle would have had to struggle for the gun, being much the stronger of the two. That he had been fatally wounded and then opened the door to escape, with the gun in his hand, and then collapse and die on the pavement seemed far fetched. There remained I knew, no possibility, that Isabel could be retried; no matter what fresh evidence might present itself. English law was wedded to the doctrine of autrefois acquit; autrefois convict. This was Norman

French my early legal studies at Police College had told me, for what the Americans called double jeopardy. If a defendant had once been put in danger of conviction by a competent court to try him/her for a criminal offence, then that was it. Once was enough. Convicted or acquitted he could not be tried again for the same offence. Even if he/she subsequently admitted to having done the deed. So Isabel could never again be tried for the murder of Henry Earle. She was free.

And so life went on. The criminals in North London continued to commit their crimes. I and my men continued to try to prevent them and, if we could not, to find them, and to get them convicted. It was a disappointment to me when, shortly after the end of the Isabel Earle trial, DC Trevor Hughes came to see me and explained that he had had an offer he could not refuse to pursue a legal career in a solicitor's office somewhere in Surrey. He was a bit obscure as to where and exactly what his new job was, but I realised that his mind was made up, and that there was nothing I could say to change it. Young Trevor had always been rather a superior sort of man for a cop, given to quoting poetry and all sorts of things which had justified his nickname of "The Professor". And so I thought no more about the sad and intriguing case of the murder trial which went wrong; until some years later, when I had almost forgotten the whole thing, when I unexpectedly received a package through the internal mail. It was from the officer in charge of a murder investigation at Richmond. It enclosed an unopened letter labelled "To Detective Chief Inspector Hollingsworth, Shoreditch; to be opened only after my death". The writing looked faintly familiar but I could not recognise it. The document inside the envelope was headed "Confession". Once I had read it I dropped everything else and went at once to Richmond.

Canst thou not minister to a mind diseased,
Pluck from the memory of a rooted sorrow,
Raze out the rooted troubles of the brain
And with some sweet oblivious antidote
Cleanse the stuff'd bosom of that stuff
Which weighs upon the heart?

MACBETH

Chapter FOUR

Penrhiw was undoubtedly the grandest house in the small mining village of Oakdale, in South Wales where I grew up. My father was the Chief Engineer at the local colliery and a qualified Civil Engineer, with a degree and letters after his name to prove it. It all gave me perhaps, an inflated idea of my own importance, as well as that of my family, in a small community. But it also gave me high aspirations to do well in life. Luckily I had a good brain and did well at school, qualifying for Hengoed, the nearby and prestigious Grammar School, which was the goal, of all the ambitious mothers in the neighbourhood for their daughters. I found the work within my capabilities, and was sometimes even among the top girls in my class. So the time came to decide what I should do in life. Flirtations were not of course in order. Love and marriage would have to wait for at least the start of a successful career, but of course for a young girl it was never quite out of mind, and I knew that I took after my attractive parents at least a little. One of the family friends in Borth-y-Gest was the local doctor, Dr Williams, who had qualified at St. Bartholomew's Hospital in London, and that was where I set my sights for a profession and for the necessary training.

But you have to remember that this was way back in 1946; the war was just over. Food was still rationed. So were clothes

117

and any poor young woman getting married had the greatest difficulty in getting any kind of a trousseau together. More importantly, it meant for me that all the men were coming back to civilian life from the Forces of the Crown. Getting back to try to pick up the threads of their careers after the disruption of war. So the competition for places in medical school at all the London hospitals was high. I could have thought of Cardiff Hospital, which would have been much easier to get into, but the best doctors were trained at the great London teaching hospitals and for me that meant that nothing else would do. And so it was that on a bright day in April of 1947, just 18 years old, and by today's standards very unsophisticated, I found myself in an austere waiting room at Bart's Hospital in West Smithfield in London, clutching the folder containing all my various certificates of attainment in the scholastic fields of South Wales. I was waiting to go into the presence of that all-important figure Dr Henry Farringdon, the Tutor of Admissions.

At last the door opened, the previous interviewee, a man, came out with a smile of satisfaction on his face and it was my turn. The great man asked the sort of questions I was prepared for. And then went on to ask more searching questions that obviously must have seemed important to him. "Do you come from a Medical Family?"

"Well my father was a Civil Engineer..." greeted with a blank stare... "but my uncle is Arthur Ruthyn-Jones FRCS, FRCOG of Harley Street and a Gynaecologist." This was greeted with a much friendlier smile. And so it went on. But after an hour during which my hopes rose and fell, he put down his pen and said:

"Miss Hambly, you have a very good academic record but you must understand that the pressure for places at this hospital is very great. We do really have to give precedence to our young men coming back from the forces, you see. Some of them have been fighting abroad for their country for the past six years, with their medical careers on hold for all of that time. We all have such a debt of gratitude to them. And of course, you are very young; there will be plenty of opportunities for you in the years to come – have you ever thought of taking up nursing? Or physiotherapy?"

He was being horribly patronising. He did not say "little girl" – well not quite. Nowadays one would have said that he was being terribly sexist but of course the phrase had yet to be invented in 1948. He must have seen the look of stark disappointment on my face. All of my thoughts for the past few years had been focused on becoming a great figure in Harley Street like my Uncle Arthur. But I would do it as a woman – and why not? I was sure that I could. Now the dreams of my schooldays were being dashed. And all through no fault of mine but just because of the time in which I lived. "The time is out of joint; O cursed spite…" I thought remembering my Hamlet. But now Dr Farringdon went on in a kindlier tone. After all it cannot have been very nice for him to have to dash the hopes and aspirations of this young woman in her carefully laundered crisp shirt and her freshly cleaned suit, a little too small because clothes rationing was a real problem and it had been bought by my parents at considerable sacrifice of both money and coupons.

"There is just one possibility you might like to consider if your heart is really set on medicine as a career…" He did not quite say "Why don't you just settle down and get married and have children, after all you are quite a pretty young woman and would make some man a very good wife in all probability." But fairly clearly that was in his mind. "…The Royal Free Hospital has got a very good reputation. It caters especially for women you see. Why don't you think of that hospital? I do have a friend who is the Tutor of Admissions to their medical school. I'm sure he would welcome your connection with Arthur Ruthyn-Jones, because I happen to know that Arthur was on the staff there for a short time and of course, he is very well thought of by everyone..."

And so it was that all hope was not quite dashed, and a few months later I found myself waiting for a similar interview at the Royal Free Hospital in Pond Street, London, NW3 with my clutch of certificates once more in my hands, and my hopes of becoming a doctor undiminished. The clutch of certificates was added to now, because the Royal Free Hospital had its own entrance examination and I had sat this successfully before applying for my interview. This time I was successful, and at last, embarking on a career in medicine. After the good news had been given to me, by post some days later, the next thing to do was to find myself some accommodation. Uncle Arthur was consulted. Not only did he live in London but was familiar with the hospital scene and the desirable, and undesirable things to look for. But the obvious would also be the best, or so he thought, and my father applied for me to have a room in the University of London Hall of Residence at Canterbury Hall, Cartwright Gardens. This was a reasonably short distance from the hospital, respectable, modestly priced and in everyway suitable for a young woman medical student fresh from the valleys of Wales and inexperienced in the wicked ways of the metropolis. Suitable, that is to say, in the eyes of the adult world and by the standards of the time. In reality I had a small, bare room with the bathroom and other standard offices at the end of the corridor. There was a warden whose chief object in life seemed to be to act as a guardian of the morals of the young women in her charge. As I soon discovered, special permission was required to receive any male visitor within the Hall of Residence and, of course, it was quite out of the question for any such visitor to be admitted to any but the rather uninviting public rooms of the Hall.

I moved on into the exciting life of a young medical student in a world surrounded by women. To begin with that did not matter a great deal. There was all the interest of medical lectures; the practical problems of the patients and the drama of particular, sometimes horrific cases. The teaching staff of the hospital had the usual mix between the sexes. It was only the students who were all woman. Even that was not quite correct. There were four men who for one reason or another had been admitted to the all women ranks of students because it had been in time of war. They had been exempt from military service because of individual physical infirmities. One was a paraplegic and came to lectures in a wheelchair and the other three had disabling but less serious deformities. But they did not amount to much of a male catchment area for the 84 young women students there were. And I had been elected as the Social Representative for my year. Why, I was never sure, since it was not really my nature to put myself forward. But it had happened. So it was my lot to help to organise the Christmas Dance, among other things. And how did one do that with such a lack of male talent to call on? Well of course some of the others had boyfriends and the boyfriends had friends of their own and there were also brothers of boyfriends; and in the end it went off very well.

As the time passed I found that the study of medicine was beginning to fascinate me. Work became compulsive. Of course I also knew how much it meant for my parents and family that I should do well and Uncle Arthur continued to take a great interest in all I did. He and Auntie Phil adopted their niece almost as a daughter. The restrictions of my Hall of Residence meant that late nights were very difficult for me. Almost unbelievably in the enlightened customs of today; every resident had to be in by 10 pm. This was still 1948 after all. There was to be a rapid change in social mores, but not yet. Of course in the war years many young girls had gone out of their way to provide friendship and rather more, for all our young men in the forces. After all they were fighting for our lives. I had had a much older boyfriend who was a fighter pilot. One of the few, who had developed a great crush on me at 16, but it had all been very innocent. My father had seen to that. So when I acquired some boyfriends in London, and started going out for an evening it involved talking to an understanding Auntie Phil – and spending a night on the Consulting Room examination bed in Harley Street, where there was no spare bedroom.

And so my years as a medical student passed, happily, busily and not without some romance. There was the very nice young barrister, Tam Pearse, who had been brought along to a party at the Royal Free by my friend Anne Sainsbury, and who had taken a liking to me, and I to him. He had even invited me to a Commem. Ball at his old college at Oxford, University College. It was the oldest college in any university he proudly explained to me. Ancient rumour had it that the College had been founded by King Alfred. In between burning the cakes, presumably. Although this was now doubted, the point had been the subject of a great case in the Court of King's Bench in the

17th Century, when a full court consisting of no less than five judges, had solemnly pronounced that it was true, thus enabling the college to benefit from an important bequest. But there were other claims by other notable colleges at Oxford, Merton and Balliol, to be the oldest and their historians had managed to cast doubt on the King Alfred legend. Nowadays, Tam explained to me, the college preferred to base its claims on more certain history. The grant by one William, Bishop of Durham for the foundation of a residence for 12 scholars at Oxford in 1249. Now it was June 1949 and the Commem. Ball was to celebrate the seventh hundred anniversary of the "second foundation" of the college since no one quite liked to abandon the charming idea that the real benefactor was Alfred himself. But what was I to wear? Where should I stay the night? Tam airily explained that there was no problem at all. The Ball went on all night and ended with breakfast, which would be followed by the customary excursion in a punt on the River Cherwell – and after that? Why then he would be happy to drive me back to London in time for duty, well perhaps just a little late, at the Royal Free Hospital. And so I managed to get permission from the hospital to be a little late for duty on 23rd June, without quite explaining the full facts behind my request to be just a little late for duty that day.

And so I went to the ball – and it was wonderful and next morning as I lay in the bottom of a punt moored alongside the banks of the "Char" in a very close embrace with Tam I wondered about qualification as a doctor. I wondered about the celibate life I led, as the sun rose and shone down giving a dappled light across the floor of the punt, over my legs with my lovely ball gown thrown carelessly high above, my own legs themselves closely intertwined with those of Tam; but ambition still burned bright. Anyway Tam was at the start of his own career at the Bar. He confessed that he was earning very little. The Dock Brief, which was his principal source of revenue, still only paid him a guinea a time, however long the case might last. Even in 1948 that wasn't very much and certainly not enough basis for earnings sufficient to support a wife. Tam Pearse had to remain a lovely memory. I had to get on with my career. I was not to see Tam again for many years – and then quite by chance.

The progression through medical school involves various academic landmarks. I passed my first MB at the end of my first year. Many hospitals granted exemption from this exam for those who had done sufficiently well in their Higher School Certificate as I had. But not the Royal Free. Nothing was made very easy for us but I remembered how lucky I was to be there at all and passed the exam anyway. And then there followed the second MB at the end of my third year. Then in due course I passed my final exams and became Dr Mary Hambly M.B., M.R.C.P. What a wonder it was to go home to Oakdale and receive a loving welcome from my parents and the admiring looks of all the girls from that small mining village, now many of them married and with children. And then I did my "house jobs" as a Houseman and a further six months as a Casualty Officer. Now I was being paid real money for the work even if it was not exactly riches it meant that I could get a share in a flat in the Gloucester Road area with two other girls. I had to decide what I wanted to do – should I become a GP like Dr Williams or should I make an effort to obtain higher qualifications as a consultant; and if so as what kind of consultant? Somehow I did not fancy becoming a gynaecologist, like Uncle Arthur. I had always been attracted by the lectures we had had on psychiatry. The human mind and its various ailments intrigued me. I decided that the first thing to do, was to obtain a Diploma in Psychiatric Medicine. It was not a very difficult exam to pass and I did pass it with honours. The obvious hospital to aim for, in view of my ambitions was the Maudesley Hospital in Denmark Hill, just opposite King's College. It was the only hospital specialising only in psychiatry at that time in the whole of London. I managed, with a good bit of help from Uncle Arthur, to obtain a further House job there. I was on my way to becoming a Consultant Psychiatrist.

Many of my friends thought I was myself quite mad, and that I should have aimed for some more usual and less demanding branch of medicine, because it was quite unusual to be a woman psychiatrist. There was only one other, in the whole of the hospital. It was a pity that she was quite elderly (at least 50) dressed like a man; and looking decidedly fierce. In fact she turned out to be very nice, but I thought her to be old fashioned in more things than her appearance. She was certainly one of the old school in her attitudes to psychiatry. Of course you have to remember that it was still a very new branch of medicine at that time. We had all been taught of the main divisions of psychiatric diagnosis and treatment. On the one hand there was psychosis, real insanity or substantial disease of the mind; and there was the possibly more curable, neurosis – divided into anxiety neurosis, hysteria and obsessional neurosis. And there again there was a clear difference, since in hysteria anxiety was largely absent. This intrigued me since after all it was accepted that hysteria could be the cause of a large number of physical symptoms ranging from paralysis of the limbs to blindness, deafness, inability to write, lapses of memory and even paralysis of the limbs. So why should anxiety be absent? When after all anxiety could itself be the cause of so many similar symptoms? I became particularly fascinated with one type of hysteria, that which caused the condition commonly known as "shell shock". It was only just being appreciated that shell shock was a psychiatric condition at all. In the 1914/1918 war it was not recognised as such. Some of our unfortunate troops suffering, it was later agreed, from shell shock were shot, for refusing their duty to go back into the trenches after periods of rest, for further exposure to enemy shells. Of course this could, and did, appear cowardly, unless a true psychiatric state was accepted. In the majority of cases at that time it was not. This was in spite of the earlier views of the great, almost the first of all psychiatrists, Sigmund Freud.

Freud had started his work with the beliefs of the medical world of the nineteenth century well drilled into him. These, until recently had been that hysteria only affected women not men. The very word came from the Greek *hustera* meaning womb, and the Greeks believed that hysteria had a purely physical cause – it resulted they believed, from a misplaced uterus. It was not until Freud, working in conjunction with the Frenchman Charcot, that it was recognised that men too, could be affected by hysteria; and it was only then that any real progress began to be made. The discovery that strong emotion was the usual provoking cause of hysteria was not generally accepted for many more years. Although there were still some die-hards in the medical world who clung to the outmoded belief that "shell shock does not exist", in general now it was accepted that it did and that it even had a brand new medical name "Post Traumatic Stress Disorder (PTSD)". The usual treatment was reassurance and drugs played little part. However it was generally recognised that doctors should not be too sympathetic to hysterical patients. Those who were unable to walk through hysteria, and there were many well-authenticated cases of this, should not be provided with a wheelchair; those who fell to the ground should not be helped up but the nursing staff should insist they got up of their own accord – or stayed there. This apparently harsh attitude was only a recognition that hysteria was itself likely to be persistent unless the patient him or herself, provided the cure. The important thing was to discover the cause of the trouble and to resolve it if possible. Medication had little part to play.

Startling examples of effective treatment for hysteria were provided by the cases in which it had caused partial paralysis. A senior consultant at the Maudesley was Dr Henry Sparrow and I was fascinated to watch his treatment of Captain Cuthie Denholm, a captain in the 8th King's Royal Irish Hussars. This patient had had a very "good war" in the accepted parlance of the post-war years. He had been through North Africa and had then fought up through Italy until he had been caught by an exploding German 88mm shell. It caught the edge of the Comet tank in whose turret he was standing. Amazingly he had escaped without physical damage although his radio operator, sitting just below him, had been killed. His right leg was paralysed from the thigh down. Extensive examination had revealed no sign of damage apart from some fairly minor cuts from a piece of flying metal, which had soon healed. Nothing could be done to heal the mental damage which was thought to be the cause of the trouble. Different psychiatrists had tried different remedies. Drugs were not the answer, not only because of the risks of dependence upon them, but because they did not often prove to be effective. That, at least was the view of Dr Sparrow. Others, of course, had tried the effects of various barbiturates as well as the so-called "truth drug" on shell-shocked patients. An intra-venous injection of

Sodium Amytal which would relax the patient so that he would be unable to tell lies. Some thought that this might be successful if the patient was in fact acting out a lie; if he really was scared stiff of returning to the lines of battle and the shell shock symptoms were part of an act.

But no drug could turn a coward into a brave man. And Captain Denholm was no coward His M.C. was testimony enough for the courage he had displayed, in the long campaigns he had fought through. So other psychiatrists had tried other methods. There had been long and careful efforts to discover the long forgotten experience of his childhood which might somehow have been revived and be the present cause of the paralysis of his leg. All had failed. But was it possible that Captain Denholm M.C. had become a coward after all? Had the effect of a long drawn out campaign through North Africa in both retreat and triumphant advance and then on to the beaches of Salerno and up through the length of Italy had some undreamed of long-term effect? Such a possibility would involve the proposition that his present condition was all a fake, and that was not to be contemplated according to Dr Sparrow. But where did you draw the line, I wondered between a conscious act to avoid doing further duty; and an unconscious act, which was provoked by the same mentality, but came unbidden and uncontrolled? Perhaps I should soon find out.

To preserve the essential confidence between patient and psychiatrist, I and the only other young doctor who was doing a third "house-job" in psychiatry, were watching the treatment, but concealed behind an observation window in an adjoining ante-room. Fascinated we watched and listened. Captain Denholm, was in pyjamas and dressing gown and seated in a hospital wheelchair, with his right pyjama trouser leg rolled up to above his knee. He was a good looking, well-built young man of about 28, now staying miraculously calm except for the slight twitch of his left hand hanging down at his side. We watched Dr Sparrow carefully draw a thick black line with a surgical crayon, round the leg just below the knee.

"Do you feel this prick?" he asked as he stuck in a pin three times just above the line.

"Yes."

"How many times?"

"Three times."

"Do you feel anything now?" and he stuck the pin in a further four times just below the line.

"No, I can't feel anything at all."

"Well, I'm now going to draw a second line two inches lower down your leg, and then I'm going to rub in special jelly called Zylocaine into the space between the two lines. You must know that the jelly will chill your leg a little so that you know that it is there. It has no other purpose but tomorrow, when the anaesthetic has worn off, the feeling, movements and all sensations, will have returned to your leg in the space between the two lines. It is not the jelly which will have done this. Its only purpose is to concentrate your mind on that particular part of your body. It is your mind which will have conquered your body."

"And you believe that?" asked Captain Denholm incredulously.

"I not only believe it; I know it," replied Dr Sparrow. "Now think no more about it, get on with your book, and I'll see you again tomorrow."

And so it proved. Once more we watched as the patient's leg was exposed. The pin was stuck in three times first above and then below the two lines that Dr Sparrow had drawn the previous day, and he asked, each time very calmly:

"Did you feel that?"

"Yes."

"How many pricks?"

"Three."

"Quite sure?"

"Certain."

"And were the second three pricks any different from the first three?"

"No, they felt just the same – quite painful."

"So your mind has conquered your body as it always will."

After that day's treatment was completed Dr Sparrow spent some time with Harry Dunning and me discussing the case. He explained his own views that whatever it might appear, the real cause of the problem was something in Captain Denholm's past, probably his remote past and quite outside his present memory. It might eventually be necessary to deal with that problem, or it might not. Severe cases of hysteria causing paralysis or even total loss of speech, very often were resolved very rapidly. It might be that this was caused by the resolution of a severe problem causing the disaster in question. It might be however that the treatment he had just commenced would not finish at its appointed time it might be sooner or just possibly later although he did not expect this; we should have to wait and see. At two inches a day, going down a calf measuring 20 inches would take 10 days. But he hoped for a sudden end to the acute part of the problem sooner than that.

In the result he proved to be wrong on that score although ultimately right as he had predicted. He went on relentlessly from day to day, until the line was drawn round the whole sole of the foot, and the pin, stuck into the big toe five times, had been correctly counted. Each day the area which reacted to the relentless pricking of the pin, was extended to include the new section of leg. Each day the patient denied any sensation when the pin was stuck in, quite hard, into the area of leg below the lower of the black bands. Not only did he deny that he felt anything, but he gave no sign whatever that he had. In the higher areas, which were duly and relentlessly tested, he showed the obvious, involuntary twitch of his face at the pain; but below the line there was no sign. His face remained impassive; it was motionless throughout.

So now came the testing time. He correctly counted five pricks of the pin into his right big toe. Dr Sparrow then said:

"And now you are going to get up, out of your wheel chair – you won't be needing that anymore now. I'll just give you a hand to stand up and then hand you over to a physiotherapist, who will help you back to bed. Please don't lean on the poor girl too much as you are rather a heavy man and physios have been known to get severe back problems themselves, when patients have suddenly collapsed upon them. Before the end of the day you can go for a walk, as long as you like, and have a look round this wing of the hospital and you can use a stick. I will have one sent to you. Tomorrow we shall take the stick away and you will be on your own. I hope your discharge from the hospital will be very soon after that but I shall continue to see you quite frequently as an out-patient until we have finally cleared up the root of the matter."

Captain Denholm looked decidedly puzzled but I noticed that he did not seem to need much help from Dr Sparrow in getting up from the examination couch; nor did he lean at all heavily upon the young physiotherapist who came in quickly in answer to his summons.

And so my own training and experience towards the coveted status of Consultant Psychiatrist progressed. I was already a Batchelor of Medicine and Member of the Royal College of Physicians (M.B.,M.R.C.P.) which exams I had passed with great pride, (and with first Class Honours). I obtained my Diploma of Psychiatric Medicine. I became a Registrar at the Maudesley, being only the second woman to have done so, and prepared for my higher exams, my Fellowship of the Royal Colleges of Medicine and of Psychiatry. I wondered what should be the subject for my thesis and decided to take a considerable chance – and to be original – original for a medical exam that is. I had always been fascinated by the various indications of mental illness to be found in the works of William Shakespeare and decided that they should be the subjects of my thesis. It was taking quite a chance because it would depend upon my examiners having at least a working knowledge of the Bard – and why should they? But at least it was important that I should be fired with enthusiasm for my subject and this I certainly was so that I decided to "give it a go".

I suppose that the most obvious example of madness in Shakespeare's works is in Hamlet, closely followed by the madness of King Lear and Lady Macbeth. Hamlet is appalled by the apparition of his father, and the news that his uncle has murdered him in order to seize the throne of Denmark and then immediately to fall into the arms of his mother. It is not surprising that Hamlet should become deranged. Not surprising that his mind should be so full of thoughts of revenge that he should forget his own deep love for Ophelia. Not even too surprising that, in order to put his plans into execution he should feign madness. As he says, "I am but mad North/North West: when the wind is Southerly I know a hawk from a handsaw"... but what real mental condition afflicted him? What was the real mental state of King Lear? Could either of them have been suffering from a kind of shell shock something like hysteria?

I must have been lucky, and my examiners at least reasonably up in the works of the great Shakespeare because it was well received. I achieved my ambition of qualifying as a Fellow of the Royal College of Psychiatrists and then became a

Psychiatric Registrar and at last a Junior Consultant at my own Hospital. Now I was enjoying treating real patients, suffering from every known mental illness. I had some success with those which had been classified as neuroses – hysteria in particular. A lot of my own treatment I classified to myself as Applied Humanity. Try to understand the patient; find out his or her background, although most of my patients were indeed women. So I thought that perhaps it was understandable that the doctors of the past had believed that only women could suffer from hysteria. Above all the psychiatrist needed to find out the cause of it all. I had to talk to them, try to be their friend, in time their confident. Try to find out what had caused it all whether the main symptoms were some defects of speech such as a stammer; some impairment of movement which like Captain Denholm's leg might amount even to partial paralysis, or an irrational phobia such as a sudden fear of the water by a young woman who had previously been a very keen swimmer. There was always a precipitating event although it might be long past and for that reason very difficult to drag up from the vaults of the patient's memory in order to be exorcised by patient discussion. Exorcised, yes, rather like the spells cast by some witch of the past. William Shakespeare would have approved. In my thesis the witches in Macbeth had been more than foretellers of the future and much more arbiters of fate for the events of the tragedy. In real life I found that quite often there was also a witchlike figure, be it a soured aunt or an embittered friend, whose influence had been the cause of serious psychiatric symptoms. Although the ancient Greeks had been ludicrously wrong in thinking that mental illness was only to be found in women, inevitably many of them found it more congenial to be treated by a woman than by a man. So I became something of a success; and even acquired some private patients.

My relaxations tended to the serious as well. I became interested in the law. Its relationship with psychiatry was considerable. There was the need for a Court Order before a person could be certified as insane, and there were the mental aspects involved in most serious crimes, and all of those which involved an element of intent in the person accused. I joined the Medico-Legal Society and started to attend their meetings at the Royal Society of Medicine. Here I met an interesting young solicitor from North London, Peter Jarrold, already a partner in his firm. And I also met Tam Pearse again who I had not seen for several years. We decided that this, was not that we had not liked each other. We had. At the start of our respective new careers there had not been much time for romance and it had seemed to both of us that the career must come first. Perhaps now things might be a little different, I wondered as he and I and Peter Jarrold sat drinking a coffee before the start of a lecture on "Jack the Ripper – was he really the Duke of Clarence – the psychological fit?" Peter was telling us all about a fascinating case that his firm had just taken on involving the capital murder of her husband, by his firm's client the former wife, now struck dumb by what she had done. We discussed the possible terrible result of a conviction for her, and the need for a change in the law. It was quite wrong that just six classes of murder should be singled out for exemption from the new general rule that a conviction for murder was no longer subject to the compulsory passing of a sentence of death. And what was the logic in singling out the six classes of murder, which still attracted a compulsory hanging? One of these was the commission of a second or subsequent murder and that seemed reasonable enough, if one was going to retain the death penalty at all. The murder of a policeman might be justified on the grounds that the police did a wonderful job, ran far more risk of being murdered than most of us, and deserved a special protection. But did this always apply? The Homicide Act 1957 was quite categorical Peter explained. "But is that logical?" I demurred. "What if, as in your present case, the murder was committed by a wife upon her husband in the course of a domestic row?" I asked.

"There are simply no exceptions to the exception," Tam explained.

"Then the law is an ass, a idiot," I replied.

"I am afraid that it sometimes is," he said ruefully.

"Even worse," I went on, the bit between my teeth. "...You say that murder with the use of a firearm is always capital murder, but that murder with the use of poison is not – what on earth is the logic of that? Is it not far more likely that a poisoning, which has to be intentional or it would not be murder, will be as the result of a carefully premeditated act?"

"I have to accept the truth of that," they both agreed.

It came as no great surprise to hear that Peter had decided to brief Tam as counsel for Isabel Earle, his client in the most important case he had yet handled. The one he had just been telling us about. But I was surprised and delighted when Peter rang me up to say that Tam had suggested that I was obviously the right Consultant Psychiatrist to be instructed to act for the defence, to examine Isabel Earle and to prepare a report of my findings. This was in view of the work he knew I had already done on hysterical aphonia. This rare condition, being literally struck dumb as the result of a traumatic event, had occasionally been found in cases of shell shock and I had written a paper on the subject as well as an article in the "Lancet", so it was reasonable enough. But I was young and inexperienced when compared with the two psychiatrists whose reports for the

Crown I now read with interest. Perhaps they had never treated a case of shell shock I mused. Their reports did not even consider a connection between the violence of the shooting which had taken place, the danger that Isabel Earle must herself have been in, or the jarring shock of the bullet wound to her own thigh. In any event they merely stated that after an examination of her, they had come firmly of the conclusion that she was insane. So insane as to come under the famous MacNaughton Rules which required that at the time of the act in question, if she were to escape the hangman's noose, she must either not have know what she was doing or must not have known that what she did was wrong.

Somehow I doubted that Isabel had not known what she was doing from what little I already knew of her. There already seemed to be some of the classic symptoms of my shell shock patients, as well as background circumstances which were not so very dissimilar. It could be said of course, that the background circumstances were mostly of her own making. But I was not concerned with morals or legal distinctions of right and wrong; surely the effect of the two kinds of shock might be the same? To be sure I should of course, have to see my patient and conduct my own examination of the lady. I 'phoned up Peter and two days later found myself within the rather grim and forbidding precincts of Holloway Prison.

A friendly Senior Wardress made the arrangements for me. I could see Isabel in an interview room and on my own if I insisted – but, she was after all a dangerous woman, one waiting trial for capital murder. There would have to be a wardress outside the door which must itself be open. I had to agree to this. My own involvement in a case of capital murder was far beyond anything I had done before. I usually saw patients – and in medical terms Isabel had to rate as a patient – but she had given no consent to being examined. Peter Jarrold had explained to me that no consent was needed because he was acting on behalf of Isabel and could give it for her. But I was not quite convinced, after all Peter was a lawyer and not a doctor, and the doctor/patient relationship was, surely a matter for me rather than for him? In any event I was only examining her and there could be no question of my giving her any treatment. And so I sat behind a desk, equipped with a bell that I should ring if there was the slightest cause for alarm, and waited for the strangest examination I had yet made.

I reflected on functional dysphonia, it was a comparatively rare complaint. Was it an extreme form of this that Isabel was suffering from? I believed from all I had heard so far, that it might be. I knew that of those suffering from dysphonia in Great Britain the large majority had no structural abnormality of the larynx such as a vocal chord polyp, nodule or papilloma, nor any sign of real paralysis. The cause was purely functional. Usually the result of some form of shock, and that the majority of sufferers, apart from those suffering with shell shock itself, were women. But I knew that a provisional diagnosis without even seeing the patient was dangerous. I knew also that two experienced psychiatrists had reached a totally different conclusion after conducting their own examination of the patient. But how much had they really known of hysterical aphonia, I wondered, how sympathetic had they really been? After all they were instructed on behalf of the prosecution and might they not have the idea, as almost everyone else on the prosecution side seemed to have, that she was a danger to the public and should be under lock and key?

And then the door opened and there she was. The drab prison uniform, the hair pulled back in a severe bun, could not conceal that she was a good-looking young woman. I knew that she was 27 and noticed that her one adornment was a gold wedding ring on her ring finger. Of course she was quite right to wear the formal recognition of her former married state as a widow. And of course it made no difference that it was alleged against her that she was only a widow because she had killed him. What would I have done had I been in her shoes? I wondered for a moment but I could reach no conclusion. After all I wasn't even married and it would be quite wrong to think of Tam Pearse in this connection, although the recent renewal of out friendship seemed to be progressing fast. After all we had both now achieved some success in our chosen professions – so?

"Please sit down," I said and she did.

"I am acting on your behalf; I am on your side. I have been instructed by your solicitor to examine you and to try to decide what, if anything, is wrong with you medically – do you understand this?"

She remained silent but there was understanding in the large eyes of the darkest blue. Then after what seemed to be a thoughtful pause she gave a distinct nod of her head.

"Try to say yes if that is what you mean."

But she only shook her head.

"Have you ever experienced any loss of speech, or any other bodily function before?"

She shook her head decidedly.

"I am going to give you a pen and a notebook and I want you to write down in your own words, exactly what happened on the day that you were arrested. Do you remember picking up a gun?"

She stayed silent but picked up the pen and wrote in rather a childish hand on the pad the words "I only remember him saying he was leaving me for Irene Barret."

"What do you remember next after that?"

Once more she picked up the pen and wrote, "The next thing I knew was that I was sitting down in the hall with a bad pain in my leg and the house was full of policemen."

Well at least it was a start. I had established a line of communications. What more could I do? The obvious next step would have been to administer an injection of Sodium Amytal, otherwise known as the "Truth Drug". It is a hypnotic, and as a barbiturate its effect is also to relax the patient. To lie calls for more of an effort than to tell the truth and use of this or a similar hypnotic drug, is very often effective in revealing the truth. But I could not use it here. It required the patient's consent and it was clear that Isabel could give no such consent. The only purpose in any event would be to reveal that her silence was all a sham and that was hardly a correct thing for her own doctor to seek to achieve. I rejected the idea. But there was just one other "trick of the trade" that I thought I could get away with, since its result might be so strongly for Isabel's advantage. It was known that a sudden surprise would produce no reaction at all from a patient who was still severely traumatised; but it might well surprise a faker into crying out; and in the case of the insane, would be likely to cause them to leap away with a scream. I had come prepared; so I had a heavy medical textbook poised on the edge of my desk. I now tipped it over with my elbow while looking intently at Isabel and as if by accident; it fell to the floor with a crash. She certainly jumped. But she did not leap away and she did not cry out. So – it seemed that there was no insanity and no still existing severe shock. I decided that the result justified my own provisional diagnosis.

Further verbal questioning by me with written answers by her, revealed that she had a fairly normal background, was interested in reading and had read a surprisingly comprehensive range of books. Anyone who had read the books of Hardy and T.S. Elliot with pleasure could surely not be stupid and must be quite out of the ordinary for a North London housewife. I began to look at her with interest and respect. But still she would only give written answers. In reply to my question, "Are you sure that you cannot just tell me the answer rather than having to write it all down?" She only wrote, "I keep trying – but nothing comes – so I have to write. No one has even asked me to do this before you did just now."

Eventually I thought that she had had enough and ended the interview confirmed in my belief that here was a woman who was not faking but suffering from hysterical aphonia. The shock of the gun battle and then being wounded was sufficient cause. It would have been severely traumatic for anyone, and for Isabel the result had been that she was struck dumb. I called the wardress and left Holloway feeling that there was nothing more that I could do to confirm or deny this diagnosis. I knew from my studies that the condition was not permanent. Once the cause of the stress was over Isabel was likely to recover her speech. Probably quite suddenly. But she was still under stress. Her very life was in danger from the hangman; if and when that awful threat was past, and assuming that she still lived, then I thought that she would recover very soon. My report to Messrs Purvis and Jarrold set out my findings and my firm conviction that I was right.

I did not waver from my opinion as I watched the proceedings in court. I think that Isabel had warmed to me a little during our interview. Perhaps I was the first friendly person she had met since her arrest. Certainly the first friendly woman, I thought, as I remembered the decidedly grim-faced wardresses in Holloway Prison for Women. Now sitting in the dock and listening to the legal formalities of a trial for murder, Isabel seemed to retreat into her shell. Her face was expressionless as she listened to the frightful indictment of her life with Henry Earle, and her violent firing of the Colt .45 which had caused his death, as retailed by counsel for the prosecution. The trial proceeded and Tam Pearse started to make some very telling points for the defence. I thought that his cross-examination of Elsie Collins was excellent, and his handling of Detective Chief Inspector Hollingsworth masterly. The possibility that the fatal shot had not been intentional at all seemed to emerge as a reality. The struggle for the gun was only guess-work certainly, but it seemed very possible that it might have been the explanation for the whole tragic event. Almost any woman would feel furious in the circumstances that Elsie Collins had suggested must have immediately preceded the final events. Elsie Collins was after all a witness for the prosecution, so it was all the more helpful for the defence that she was so obviously sympathetic to the defendant. Prosecuting counsel made a speech which predictably left no room for doubt as to his view that the only verdict was "guilty as charged" or, at least with the proviso that a verdict of "guilty but insane", might be a reasonable, indeed the only, alternative.

And then Tam got to his feet and started his speech to the jury. Everyone in court listened to him with rapt attention. I thought that I noticed the effects of a "good school" and Oxford University, upon a naturally beautiful speaking voice. I detected the occasional and very faintest trace of a Devonshire accent, betraying his origins and the reason for the pronunciation of his first name. He even became a little emotional himself as he described the effect that the sudden announcement of betrayal, as given to her by Elsie must have had upon his client. He repeated his best point at the end, as he reiterated:

"No wonder she was upset, furious, members of the jury, but that is no reason for murder. And it certainly is not murder until the prosecution proves it – if they can – and they certainly can't unless they are able to exclude all other possibilities so that you, each and every one of you, are quite satisfied that no other possibility can exist – and you don't need me to tell you that you can't possibly be satisfied of that."

And Tam sat down. There was a distinct sound of applause instantly hushed by the court officials. I glanced across at the defendant. She had been sitting apparently unmoved, Looking quite calm and serene, for all the world as if all these

143

proceedings had very little to do with her. But just for a moment I saw her glance across at Tam and their eyes seemed to meet, before she looked straight to her front once more.

And then it was the turn of the judge. He seemed to be in no doubt about it all himself. He was at pains to explain to the jury that it was their decision, not his. But in spite of this he left very little doubt that his own opinion was that she was a very dangerous young woman. The two consultant psychiatrists called for the prosecution had had no doubt that she was insane. Well, an acceptance of their findings would mean that she would not hang but would "be detained during Her Majesty's Pleasure", in other words would go to Broadmoor where, of course, she would receive the right care and treatment, and no longer be any danger to the public. He did deal with my own evidence with some respect. He did not actually say "...but of course she is very young and inexperienced when compared with those called for the Crown, Doctors Harold Rathbone and John Elton." He laid heavy emphasis on their own very good qualifications and did not even mention my own experience in the particular field of hysterical aphonia. He left very little doubt that he regarded the suggestion that it might all have been an accident as fanciful, although of course he had to say, that if they believed that it was true, or even might be true, then they would have to return a verdict of "not guilty".

When the judge finished, the Jury Bailiffs were duly sworn to "keep this jury in some safe and convenient place and not to speak to them, save to ask them if they be agreed upon a verdict, nor to suffer others to speak to them while they are in your charge without the leave of the court." And they duly filed out to the "safe and convenient place", the Jury Room. I noticed that

several of them, particularly the women, glanced at he
defendant, as she still sat silent and unmoving in the dock; and
that their glances seemed to be not without sympathy.

I left court myself and made for the Coffee Room where I
saw Tam deep in conversation with Mervyn Griffith, the counsel
for the prosecution. It was still a bit of a puzzle to me: the ways
of the Bar. They were all "My Learned Friend" as far as
addressing the court was concerned, even though they might
have just met for the first time. Then they were all fiercely
opposed to each other while the trial went on; then they might in
fact turn out to be quite good friends in spite of, or could it be
because of the rivalry that existed between them? After a short
time Tam looked up and waved to me. Then he brought his
coffee over to my table and we talked about the trial; about our
earlier conversations on the intriguing subject of Isabel Earle –
and about ourselves. Tam invited me to the Summer Ball in
Middle Temple and I did not hesitate in accepting.

And then an usher came into the Coffee Room to announce
that the jury were back in court. They must have arrived at a
verdict. We all rushed back to find out what it would be.

It came as no real surprise to me to hear the question the
jury wanted to ask the judge which showed quite clearly that
they had not been convinced that Isabel was guilty of murder. So
the judge had no option but to discharge her from custody. I was
very happy to go along with the judge's request that I should be
one of the party to accompany her home and I set off in a
crowded taxi with Isabel herself and Elsie Collins and DC
Trevor Hughes. I looked around the very ordinary surroundings
of 12, Clacton Street and I noticed that Isabel seemed to relax at

once. After all it was her home and perhaps she had never expected to see it again. Elsie Collins went to her own house next door and came back with a pint of fresh milk and went to the cupboard she was obviously familiar with, to get out the tea, and then she made us all a cup, which we badly needed. Isabel started to show obvious signs of interest and awareness and agreed to come upstairs to the bedroom with me by a nod of her head. I knew how much any woman's bedroom means to her and watched with relief as Isabel put down the holdall, she had brought from prison and started to arrange her things in their familiar places. It was all very good news from a psychiatrist's point of view. I drank my tea and said that I would come back next day to arrange for some continuing treatment for Isabel. I left the house with Elsie Collins as Trevor Hughes politely held the door open for us. I knew that cases of hysterical aphonia often recovered quickly once all causes of the original stress had been removed. The opinion I had given in court had been that this was likely in Isabel's case, and I felt pretty sure that I should be prove to be correct.

The next day I made my way to Clacton Street as arranged, after my own day's work at the hospital had finished, and knocked at the door. Isabel herself opened it. She had on a pretty dress that I had not previously seen. She was wearing make-up, which of course had been strictly forbidden in prison. She looked a different person altogether and she said:

"Why, good morning Dr Hambly, how lovely to see you. Do please come in…"

The Judicial view

"Murder is the highest crime against the Law of Nature;
it occurs when a man of sound mind and of the age of discretion,
unlawfully killeth another person under the King's Peace
and with malice aforethought, either expressed by the party
or implied by the law, so as the party wounded or hurt, die of
the wound or hurt within a year and a day."

The Cyclopaedia of Law,
John Adlington Esquire, Lincoln's Inn, 1820

Chapter Five

I was now Sir Henry Scrutton, recently appointed to the position of a Judge of the High Court, and I was sitting in the judges' lodgings at Exeter as one of Her Majesty's Judges of Assize, with all the comfort and splendour which attends the holder of that office. The assize was on the Western Circuit it had just reached Exeter; after a period of two weeks in that ancient city, I should be going on for a spell in London where I should be judging only criminal cases at the Central Criminal Court, the "Old Bailey". So soon I should have a chance to see something more of my wife and family and cast my eye over the garden in our Georgian house in Edwards Square in Kensington. Not that I was without a wife on this assize. The quaint custom of Her Majesty's judges on assize was that the senior judge on that assize decreed, whether or not wives might accompany their husbands. If the senior judge happened to be a bachelor then it was likely that no wives would be allowed. But Croom-Jackson the senior judge on this assize was married and had decreed that there should be wives, and so the redoubtable Lady Croom-Jackson and my own beloved Clarissa were with us. It meant that for them they had a place in the very comfortable house provided for the judges, not too far from the cathedral and the best shopping area of Exeter. There was a cook and other servants including a butler, to organise it all. There was the

149

company of their husbands and the other judge or judges and their marshals, and the other wives

Marshals were young barristers, usually "newly called", in other words before they had even started a "pupillage" at the Bar. They were paid a small sum by the Lord Chancellor's Office, for being in effect well-educated, agreeable equerries for their judge. To fetch and carry for him, to sit beside him in court and, from their own point-of-view, to gain very valuable practical experience of how it all worked. They would listen to the cases and hear experienced counsel conduct them. I had given young Victor Watts a niece of Clarissa's and newly called to the Bar, his chance and now he sat opposite to me in my room after breakfast on the first day with the formalities of opening the assizes about to commence.

"The papers for your cases at the Old Bailey have just arrived, Uncle Henry," said Victor respectfully. "…I have been having a look at them and one of them is a very interesting case of capital murder. Regina versus Isabel Earle, a young woman who killed her husband by shooting him so she might hang…"

"A young woman who is accused of killing her husband by shooting him, don't forget, young Victor," I replied. "That is what is so important, because if she had poisoned him instead of shooting him, why then under the present law she could not hang. It does seem to be an absurd distinction to me but then I only administer the law, as best I can, I do not make it and anyway I don't suppose that she is going to admit it, because that would be rather like signing her own death warrant. It will mean that the prosecution will have to prove their case. Capital murder as you say – the jury will probably strain themselves backwards to bring in a verdict of 'not guilty' particularly as the defendant is a woman – but that will all be in two weeks' time and now we have half an hour to wait for the coach. This is Exeter and you and I and Mr Justice Croom-Jackson will all be called for, to be taken by horse-drawn coach from the lodgings and up to the cathedral to be 'churched'. You will remember that the same thing happened at Winchester; but they don't have a coach there, thank the Lord, since this one is said to be not very comfortable. The bishop will see that Croom-Jackson and I are in a proper frame of mind to administer justice in Exeter, he will ensure that we have confessed our own sins, and are suitably blessed to deal with the sins of others, before we set out on our duties to do so – so if you will forgive me I'll just have a glance at the *Times* before we set out, but don't let me stop you reading all about the murder case we have coming on in London."

And Victor dutifully pored over the papers in front of him as I caught up with the headlines. But they seemed to have nothing much of interest to tell me and I found myself reflecting on the legal career I had had so far. I was now treated as Her Majesty's Representative – one of her Judges of Oyer and Terminer and General Gaol Delivery on assize on the Western Circuit. It only meant that I had to hear the cases that came before me and decide them, and to release the prisoners waiting trial if they were found to be innocent and to deal with them appropriately if they were instead found to have been guilty of the offences with which they had been charged. It did mean that I had almost unlimited powers and would be certain to be kow-towed to by the High Sheriff of the County of Devon, the Mayor, the Aldermen and all the rest of them. It was quite difficult not to let it all get to one's head, and just as well that our wives were with us to cut it all down to size. Particularly I thought in the case of Croom-Jackson. He may have been a terror to the barristers who had to appear before him in court, but everyone knew that he was very much at the beck and call of the imperious Priscilla, his wife.

Croom-Jackson came from a long line of barristers and judges and had had no problems about entering the law as a barrister by way of the first step which was to become a pupil. My own family had little in the way of legal connections. However the last Chairman of the Bar Council, Clive Vick had just been appointed to the High Court Bench and happened to be also a Governor of the school I had once attended as a boy. Although I did not know him at all personally. I steeled up my courage and telephoned the great man at the number of the Royal Courts of Justice in London where I knew he was sitting trying a case of defamation of character which had been in all the headlines. He was quite charming and at once asked me to come and see him in his room in the High Court, after work had finished the next day. And we got on very well and he promised to do what he could since he knew that a friend of his, who could usually be relied upon to help if asked. He managed to achieve a great deal, because a few weeks later I found myself sitting at a desk in the corner of a large room at 1, Paper Buildings, The Temple. My new Pupil Master, Mr Teddy Hamilton-Jenkins sat at a much larger desk in the centre of the room reading his brief for an "accident" case before Mr Justice Thornton for the next day. And so my new career had been fairly launched and I followed my new Master in the Law and tried to note his technique. Teddy was an awesome advocate. The terror of any lying witness who was "called for the other side". Of course there were "tricks of the trade" which I noted for my own future use. "If the other party has sworn any affidavit during the course of the proceedings before the trial – just have it in mind when he gives his own evidence in chief, at the actual hearing. If there is any significance variance between the two, even if it is a matter of little consequence, then you may have the chance of discrediting him. First nail him down to what he has just said in court..." and very soon I was to hear the great man doing exactly this:

"Mr Barnaby, you have just told the court that it was raining slightly at the time of the accident on 7th July?"

"Yes, and so it was."

"Are you really certain of that?"

"Quite certain."

"Really sure?"

"I've just said so."

"But didn't you once say quite the opposite?"

"Certainly not."

"Are you really quite sure? Usher, please hand the witness the original of the affidavit he swore on the 21st January last year, in support of his application for Discovery of Documents, before Master Hewitt," and the document was duly handed to him.

"Now look at that affidavit… is that your signature at the end? Where you swear that the contents of your affidavit are true?"

"Yes."

"Now just read out what you swore to in Paragraph 15 of the affidavit?"

"On 7th July I was in no hurry and driving carefully, it had been raining but this had now cleared…"

"Stop there Mr Barnaby, you have just sworn on oath that it was raining slightly so please just tell my Lord – were you lying then – or are you lying now?"

And of course there could be no answer to that. It seemed to work a treat. Of course the judge knew that memory was fallible and that the witness had not been intentionally lying at all, but at least a lot of doubt had been thrown upon his accuracy. One more case a victory for Teddy Hamilton-Jenkins. I carefully stored it up for future use when the occasion should be right for me. As well as useful tricks of the trade of course, there was a wealth of practical knowledge. From the very simple knowledge of where the various courts were situated; to the form of address for the various judges, magistrates, coroners and tribunals before whom we appeared; to the right way to talk to clients and gain their confidence. It was very simple, effective learning by example from a master craftsman in the art of presenting and winning cases in court.

But all of that was a long time in the past. I had graduated from my own pupillage; I had started to do my own cases. From the very insignificant case for the recovery of a trade debt before a Registrar in West London County Court to minor crime in the Magistrates Court, then to grander criminal cases at the Old Bailey or at London sessions in Newington Causeway. More important and better-paid cases. I seemed to have inherited a bit of the gift of the gab from my father, veteran Alderman and former Sheriff of the Exeter Council, which boasted a sheriff because it was "The City and County – of the City of Exeter". Perhaps even helped by some inherited strains from my mother whose Welsh ancestors had included many a firebrand Methodist minister preaching to the faithful in the valleys of her native South Wales. Whatever the reasons I warmed to my new profession and found the work absorbing. Chiefly I am sure, because it was all about people, my fellow human beings and their very personal problems. Some difficult, some bizarre, some just horrid: but all full of interest because they were about people. Even if some of the clients were themselves a little bit horrible, I liked meeting them. Let me confess I was just a little bit pleased with the deference that they showed to me as their counsel – the specialist, their own solicitor had chosen from all the hundreds there were in practice at the Bar at that time. I began to be quite good at the job and had a successful run of cases in particular in the field of medical negligence, when trying to obtain compensation for the ruined lives that could result from just a few moments carelessness on the part of a surgeon or the effects of a wrong diagnosis by a clinical doctor.

In time I became rather more successful, and this meant that I could marry and have a family. There was no doubt who it would be if she agreed and luckily for me, she did. I "took silk" soon afterwards and became a QC Then there followed some years of hectic practice, hard work, long hours, much travelling but tremendous interest; the flushes of victory and the agonies of unexpected defeat. A successful practice meant that the hardships of my early days at the Bar were relieved but of course, at the cost of a disrupted home life. I remember on returning home after a few days spent at Bodmin Assizes, a remote spot and about as far away from home as I ever went, where I had an embarrassingly devoted client, a tearful note from my seven-year-old daughter. It read: "Daddy, today I was 7. It is my birthday – where was you? luv Claire." My busy life was bound to involve some sacrifices, and I was soon able to give some solace to Claire by way of a trip to the zoo. It was difficult to explain to her that I could not order my own life, as I had such an important part in deciding upon hers, but the hard truth was that what I did, had to depend very much on my work load and a well paid brief at Bodmin Assizes from a good client could not be ignored when I had to consider important things such as the payment of school fees. I had very little doubt or hesitation when offered the great honour of promotion to the High Court Bench.

Acceptance of this offer meant a steady and certain income and assured pension, more time at home and less intensive work – and the honour of knighthood. But it also meant giving up the life I had come to love, the rough hurly burley of practice at the Bar with all the travelling, the conferences with clients, the discussions of the cases with my solicitors and the lay clients; as well as with opponents, in order to try to reach agreement on a settlement of the dispute. It meant to a large degree, the loss of the companionship that I had found among friends in Chambers, the loss of all those discussions about interesting cases in

Chambers and over lunch in the Middle Temple Hall or in the cafeteria of the Royal Courts of Justice in the Strand.

Of course there had been many compensations for the loss of the busy life of the Bar. I was still doing the same sort of work from a different perspective. What I said in court was decisive. The fate of the litigants was in my hands in civil cases. In criminal cases because of the duty of the judge to "stop" a case in which he did not believe a conviction would be safe, the fate of any defendant depended upon the will, if not the whim, of the judge who was trying the case. The ultimate result except for the rare case when the judge intervened to prevent a possible miscarriage of justice was of course in the hands of the jury. Even so the fate of the defendant depended a great deal on the way the judge summed up the case to them. He might say as often as he liked: "members of the jury, you are the only judges of fact in this case – ignore anything I may say as to the truth of the facts the prosecution need to establish, unless you agree with them…" The fact was, as the judge himself very well knew, that anything he did say, would be likely to carry the greatest weight when the jury was debating the vital issue of "guilt" or "innocence" in their discussions in the Jury Room.

I had known very well, from chats I had had with friends who had already been promoted to the Bench, that life would not be the same. That it was almost certain that I should feel a little of the loneliness of high office. That I should miss the chats with friends and opponents in the Robing Rooms. My hesitations had been brief. Whatever I was to give up would be more than counterbalanced by the security and high standing of the job of a High Court Judge. I had soon come to enjoy my newfound glory and the power that came with the job. A case of capital murder with the accused, a young woman in grave danger of being hanged was daunting. It would be the first time I had ever been called upon to do such a thing. But there was no escape and so I had just resolved to have a very careful read of the depositions and other documents in the case when Victor Watts came in to announce that the judge's coach was waiting, and Mr Justice Croom-Jackson was about to come down from his room to depart and wanted to know if I was fully robed and ready for the formalities about to be performed in Exeter cathedral. I had a final look in the mirror, adjusting my wig and my robes before descending the stairs and getting into the coach beside Croom-Jackson. The coachman cracked his whip and we were off along the narrow streets leading from the judge's lodgings to the cathedral. Built some three hundred years ago, the coach was an imposing and novel way of getting about.

"Don't know why they keep this old thing – it's about as comfortable as a tumbrel on its way to Highbury," complained Croom-Jackson.

"Tradition," I replied. "It looks very grand and it does give dignity to the occasion – besides Exeter would not be the same without its famous coach and horses."

I did think myself, that all the ceremony, all the grandeur, the wigs and gowns of the judges and of counsel appearing before them in their courts, did play a part. That any witness was just a little bit more likely to tell the truth when in a witness box in a crowded court and on oath, than he would have been on a less formal occasion.

That the trappings of a Judicial Hearing all helped just a little, to make the witnesses speak the truth.

And then with a shout from the coachman and the squealing of ancient brakes, the carriage came to a halt outside the cathedral and I looked out to see the lines of waiting Councillors and Aldermen of Exeter, the Mayor, the Sheriff and in front of them the Lord Lieutenant and the High Sheriff of the County of Devon, flanked by soldiers of the Devonshire regiment in ranks, who had just been called to attention, and were now presenting arms to Her Majesty's Judges. It was very grand, and I was impressed in spite of myself. It was after all, my first visit to the city of my birth as a judge rather than as a young barrister just visiting his parents or appearing in court. I had known it for so many years since childhood, and it was nice to know that all my "sisters and my cousins and my aunts" who still lived round about, would be reading about the cases I should soon be trying, in the columns of the *Express* and *Echo* or the *Western Morning News*. But all the ceremony and grandeur, splendid as it was, did not quite satisfy Croom-Jackson.

"No trumpeters?" he said in disgust. "It really is too bad, the war has been over for years now and a niggardly and grudging government still do not afford them as they always used to before the war."

I could remember that when I had gone on assize with my old Pupil Master, Wilfrid Fordman, judges had been received at this stage with a fanfare of trumpets, as well as all the rest of the panoply of grandeur, which must have boosted their ego still further. For myself I could not say that their absence made a lot of difference but I replied diplomatically:

159

"Well Exeter always did things well and I've no doubt we'll be getting them back quite soon – but after all, it is not all that many years since food and clothes were being rationed – and I suppose that it all does take time."

Croom-Jackson gave a snort of disgust at the very notion that he might be deprived of his trumpeters for any length of time, but then prepared for the formalities of a blessing by the bishop for our endeavours, and our own prayers, that we should indeed do justice to all men, without fear or favour. More than a formality in my case at least, since as a believer, I knew that I should need all the help I could get to come to a just decision in the multitude of cases that I should be called upon to try at Exeter. With the words of the good bishop ringing in our ears, we left the cathedral and re-entered the ancient coach. Amid more salutes and with the Devonshire regiment once more at the "present" we set off for the castle. Castles were commonly built on hills to give the defenders the physical advantage that they could rush down upon the attackers from on high, or shoot down upon them bolts, arrows, rocks, whatever. And so it was at Exeter. The coach was old and I rather expected that the horses were probably not in the first flush of youth either. They certainly seemed to need a lot of urging from the coachman, to get us up the steep hill from the High Street to the level ground in front of the castle itself. I heaved an inner sigh of relief when they had done so and Croom-Jackson and I could leave the coach to be greeted by our marshals and our clerks and conducted into our respective courts to start the business of the day.

After court we foregathered at the Lodgings for a glass of sherry before dinner. We were being joined that evening by the

High Sheriff for Devon and his lady and by the Mayor and Mayoress of Exeter; but they had yet to arrive when the sherry was first poured out.

"Reggie, I hear that you have been going over the top and making a complete ass of yourself again," said Lady Croom-Jackson.

Her husband quailed. It was well known at the Bar, and after all I had only just left practice on my appointment as a judge myself, that the Honourable Sir Reginald Croom-Jackson was a complete tyrant in court himself. But that the wife, who he adored, was in her turn something of a tyrant to him. He was not a judge to be crossed. And although few were, it was particularly true in his case. Many were the young barristers who had returned to Chambers white if not actually tearful, after falling foul of Reggie in court. Croom-Jackson had the highest possible regard for his own standing and importance. The story was told, of the occasion when some industrious but noisy, workman had been hammering on top of the roof above his head, as he sat trying a case in the Royal Courts of Justice in the Strand. At last he could stand it no longer and sent out the usher to fetch the culprit before him to answer for his sins. The usher returned with a small bedraggled looking workman, clutching the offending hammer in his hand.

"The business of this court is not to be interrupted," said Reggie pompously. "You will sit in court until the end of the day and until after the court has risen – then you can get back to your hammering and make as much noise as you like without disrupting the business of this court."

And so the small man sat right in front of the judge holding his hammer and looking defiant, until 4.15 pm when the business of the day finished, the usher shouted, "The court will adjourn." Reggie rose to his feet and bowed to counsel sitting in their row, and swept out. The little man then said loudly and triumphantly:

"Silly old bugger don't he know I'm paid by time?"

Lady Croom-Jackson spoke again:

"Reggie is it true what I've heard?"

"And what is that my dear?" quavered the tyrant of the courts.

"Why only that Mavis Bullock tells me that when you were sitting at Maidstone last week, you grounded all the aircraft at Biggin Hill? Just because you said that they were too noisy flying over your head – so you ordered them to stop flying for the rest of the day – and they did."

"Well my dear the court's business on assizes is the Queen's business and they were very noisy…"

"So it is true… Reggie you were making an ass of yourself again… that must be an abuse of your powers… to keep the Royal Air Force on the ground all that day when they must have had their own important work to do…" It did not seem to matter to Lady Croom-Jackson that this little scene was being enacted in front of me and, even worse, young Victor Watts; she was obviously enjoying herself. But then, fortunately perhaps and before poor Croom-Jackson, the tyrant of the courts had a chance to justify himself, the High Sheriff and his Lady were announced and conversation became general.

Court business was very brisk at Exeter until the last day of the assizes when the case I was trying, a lengthy and difficult one of medical negligence, collapsed because the parties managed to reach agreement on the terms of a settlement of their dispute. I was happy to make a Tomlin Order, that all further proceedings were to be stayed save for enforcing the terms of settlement, as endorsed on counsel's briefs. I then found myself back in the lodgings with time on my hands to have a look at last at the papers for my cases at the Old Bailey the following week. I looked at the case of Regina versus Isabel Earl, the one that had so impressed Victor Watts, first of all and read the depositions with growing interest.

It all seemed to be very clear. Here had been a young woman who had fallen out with her husband. There was a suggestion that he was about to leave his wife for another woman. Unfortunately it was happening all the time. But mercifully it did not often happen that the wife then picked up a loaded revolver and shot him. So far all was clear. But then the case rapidly became far from clear, because I read of her complete silence ever since the incident itself. That was certainly very unusual. Virtually always an accused person said something. Often far too much for their own good, usually to deny or to explain what had happened. Sometimes to admit it. But Isabel Earle had said nothing at all. She had apparently quite literally been struck dumb, so there had been no kind of explanation. Looking at the medical reports I saw why. Reading those of Doctors Harold Rathbone and John Elton, I noted their long experience and high qualifications as psychiatrists. They were firmly convinced that the young woman was insane within the meaning of the McNaughton Rules. These rules followed the ruling in the case of Regina versus NcNaughton decided in 1843. Up to then the harsh rule of law was that if you had committed murder and were convicted of it, then you were hanged. It substituted the merciful provision, that if you were also found to have been insane then you would escape the hangman's noose and be detained in some secure institution instead. And insanity was defined as being such a condition that the defendant did not know what he or she was doing and so did not understand "the nature or the quality of the act" or, while knowing what they were doing, nevertheless did not know that it was wrong.

So did that apply to Mrs Earle? I wondered. The two senior doctors who had given reports for the prosecution seemed to be in no doubt that the definition applied in her case. If that were so then the verdict would have to be one of "guilty but insane" and she would at least escape hanging. And I should be saved the unpleasant necessity of passing a sentence of death upon her I reflected with relief. But then there was the report filed on behalf of the defence by a Dr Mary Hambly. I noticed that although she had all the academic qualifications of the other two, they were more recent. She did not have the same long experience in the field of psychiatric medicine as they had. Even so I was surprised to read that her conclusions were quite different. I saw that she spoke of hysterical aphonia, a condition I had never heard of before, but which she said was a neurotic condition which caused a temporary dumbness only. Of course it would be for the jury to decide which of the sharply different medical opinions, should be accepted, since it was clearly not possible that they could accept them both.

My own feeling was that whatever else, here was a young woman who seemed almost certainly rightly charged with capital murder, whatever provocation there might have been. But if she had been insane at the time, then that explained it. English law did not recognise the French idea of the crime passionnel. Isabel Earle was a very dangerous woman who had wrought a terrible revenge on her husband. And what she had done once, who could say, she might well do again. My first duty as I saw it, was to make sure so far as I possibly could, that the public were protected. If Isabel Earle was convicted then she would have to hang. But if the jury accepted either of the conflicting medical opinions then in fact she would not do so. If she was judged to have been insane then it meant that I should have to send her to Broadmoor, where she would probably remain for the rest of her life. If the diagnosis of hysterical aphonia was found to be valid, then it would follow that Isabel Earle would be saved the hangman; and would be saved from Broadmoor too because it would mean that she had been acting with "diminished responsibility". It would follow that the charge would have to be reduced from murder, with its obligation that the prosecution had to prove an intention to kill, to the lesser charge of manslaughter. This in turn meant that I should have to decide upon a term of imprisonment suitable for the circumstances. Even then it would not be easy for me. What sentence of imprisonment was appropriate for a young woman, plagued by a violent husband, who was having an affair with one of her neighbours, and who was a thoroughly bad lot anyway, when things suddenly snapped? I knew that I would be much surer of the answer to that very difficult question when I had seen the lady and heard everything that everyone would have to say about her. I found it a fascinating case. It was quite unlike anything that I had ever come across before. But whatever the answer it seemed to follow that she would be put away in some secure place until any remaining danger to the public was long past. It certainly never crossed my mind that the jury might acquit her altogether.

There was another difficult legal point that I should have to decide. If the lady could not speak she could not enter a plea to the indictment when it was formally put to her at the beginning of her trial. The rule from time immemorial was that only the defendant, him or herself, could do this, and not anyone on their behalf, except in very rare cases the trial judge himself could order that a plea of "not guilty" should be recorded if the interests of justice demanded it. But only he could do that, not even her own counsel, although of course he was bound to have advised on the matter before hand. How could counsel give any proper advice, I wondered, when she could not speak and presumably had been unable to give him any account at all of what had happened? I felt sorry for the unfortunate barrister who had to defend a woman on the capital charge in these difficult circumstances, and I looked at the papers to see who it might be. T.D.F. Pearse I read. Francis Pearse it was, of course. Who like me hailed from the West Country, and always known as "Tam". "Tam Pearse, Tam Pearse, lend me your grey mare, out along, down along, out along ley…" Something about going to Widdicombe fair with Uncle Tom Cobleigh and all, I seemed to remember. Anyway it had got him his nickname. A likeable young man, I remembered, very bright, who I had once had as a junior in a fraud case about three years ago. Well, I reflected he was likely to do the case very well. But I should have to try the case very well also. I did not want Tam Pearse getting Isabel Earle off the hook by some piece of forensic skill, if the Justice of the case and the needs of the public, meant that she should be behind bars.

And what about the initial problem of how she was to enter a plea to the charges in the indictment at all? I thought about this question a good deal. After all there were not many cases where any defendant refused to say anything on arraignment. Arraignment was the technical term for the first stage of a trial for any serious crime on indictment. Before the jury were empanelled but with the judge, counsel and solicitors, all present, the charge in the indictment would be solemnly read out in a clear voice to the prisoner in the dock who would be standing up, between two restraining warders or in this case wardresses; so positioned that they could frustrate any last minute leap for freedom which the prisoner might make. I imagined the scene with the clerk solemnly intoning the words of the charge against her.

And the defendant would say nothing, because on all the reports that I had read she could not speak – unless, of course, when it actually came to it she might recover her powers of speech so as to save her own life, by saying "not guilty", with all the conviction she could muster? Well anything could happen in a case like the present one but it did not seem to be very likely. I knew that in this event the legal requirement was that a special jury should be empanelled to decide the question whether she was silent because she was "mute by visitation of God", which meant that she was physically unable to speak or "mute of malice" which meant that she could but did not want to. I saw a copy of Halsburys' Laws of England in the bookcase in the sitting room of the judges' lodgings, now empty save for me. I took down the volumes devoted to the criminal law and had little difficulty in finding the right place. I knew that I needed to refresh my mind on this unusual subject. I read:

"Accused standing mute. If the accused on being arraigned stands mute and does not answer, the judge directs a jury to be empanelled and sworn to try the issue whether he be mute of malice or by the visitation of God. If the accused has counsel, his counsel may address the jury and call witnesses to prove that he is mute by the visitation of God. If he stands mute of malice or will not answer directly to the indictment, the court may order a plea of not guilty to be entered on his behalf and he must then be tried as if he had pleaded not guilty. If the jury finds that he is mute by visitation of God, the further issue then falls to be tried, namely whether he is fit to be tried. If the accused can communicate by signs, and there is anyone who can interpret the signs to the court, or if the accused can read and write, the jury should be directed that he is fit to be tried, and he may then be arraigned and may answer by signs or by means of writing."

Well all of that seemed to be reasonably clear. But on the facts of this case I did not like it at all. In particular the possible need for empanelling a jury to try the issue of whether she was fit to plead seemed to be very awkward when there would then be the need for a second jury to decide the question of "guilt" or "innocence". I knew that it was likely that Tam Pearse would have to call his own psychiatrist as a witness. Not to do so would mean that any finding of "guilt" would mean the inevitable passing of a sentence of death, which I would have to do; there would be no escape for me. And what fanciful defence could young Tam conjure up in the absence of any explanation from his client? I thought it almost certain that he would be forced to call his doctor. And then the prosecution would be able to call theirs. That was the rule. The defence had the right to decide and it was only if they put the question of sanity into issue by calling their own doctor, that the prosecution had the right to dispute it by asking for leave to call their own medical witnesses to give evidence "in rebuttal". Well at least that was all to the good because they were quite clear that the young woman was insane. If the jury rejected the evidence of Dr Hambly, that she was not mad at all, that would mean an equally inevitable sentence that she be sent to Broadmoor. At least the public would be safe. But after all it was not only that I should like to ensure the safety of the public. The life of a young woman was at stake. The more I thought about it, the clearer it seemed to me that the best course for me, and certainly the most favourable thing for the defendant, would be to exercise my undoubted right to decide that a plea of "not guilty" be entered on her behalf. And then Croom-Jackson returned from court and I had a chance to discuss my interesting case with a judge whose experience of criminal cases was much greater than mine. And then, since the assizes had finished at Exeter, we all went home for the weekend, before the London cases started the following Tuesday at the Old Bailey.

When I came into court on that day I was surrounded by all the pomp and circumstance of the law as organised by the City of London. There were no trumpeters here either, but then I remembered that there never had been at the Old Bailey; although after all, they had the City Sheriffs in all their livery instead. They did things very well in the City, as even Reggie Croom-Jackson would have agreed. And I had to admit to myself with slight reluctance that I could not find it in me to resent in any way, the deference of the officials, the politeness of the two sheriffs of the City, with whom I should shortly be lunching, or the stentorian call from the Clerk of the Court of "All rise for Her Majesty's Judge" and the bows of counsel in their rows at the front of the court as I entered to take my seat, followed by my clerk and my chaplain. It was only when there was a case of capital murder that a chaplain was necessary. And then only if a verdict of "guilty" was returned would he be called upon to invoke the aid of the deity to have mercy on the soul of the convicted murderer after the passing of the inevitable sentence of death. I reminded myself, yet again, that I must not let it all go to my head. I was just an ordinary human being with some moderate talent, who had been lucky. And now I had to settle down and try to ensure that justice was done – and, as I reminded myself, that the public should be protected at all costs.

As everyone in court sat down after making their dutiful bows to me, I looked about and took stock of the various principal characters in the drama that was about to unfold and to occupy the next few days of my life. I noted the tall distinguished figure of Mervyn Griffith sitting immediately below me, and beside him the slightly shorter, younger, good-looking, figure of Tam Pearse; each surrounded by the attendant figures of their solicitors, their clerks and, in Mervyn Griffith case, his pupil. Then my eyes turned to the dock and I took in the slight figure there, sitting between the two grim-faced women gaolers. She was wearing a drab ill-fitting dress, provided presumably by Her Majesty's Prison for Women at Holloway. Her hair was swept back from her face. But nothing could disguise her natural beauty. Her eyes I saw, were a striking shade of blue. They were set in a face which was quite immobile and quite serene. Isabel Mary Earle might be in imminent danger of the passing of a sentence of death, which would cause that slim neck to be broken at the end of the hangman's noose, but you would never have thought so to look at her. She rose to stand at the urgings of her two wardens, as the whole court also rose while the Clerk of the Court put the words of the indictment to her. There was a complete silence as everyone waited to hear her reply. And there was none.

"Put it to her again," I said to the Clerk of the Court.

And he did so with exactly the same response. The defendant looked calm, untroubled and somehow, as if she had been not on trial for her life, but enjoying a quiet, not unhappy reflection on a pleasant topic and on a calm occasion. This was very unusual. It had never happened to me before; luckily I was prepared for it. As I had decided I ordered that a plea of "not guilty" be entered. Everyone looked relieved that there would not have to be a separate issue on the subject. And the trial commenced, and went on its interesting and amazing course, until we adjourned for the day. I sent the jury away with the usual stern admonition that they should speak of the case to nobody, save to themselves and should not be influenced in any way by anything that they might happen to read in the newspapers, or hear on the radio or TV. Because the case inevitably had captured the public imagination. The beautiful young woman, whose picture, had already received wide publication. The circumstance that she had been struck dumb and so could not give her own version of what had happened so as to defend herself had been seized upon by the press as a particularly poignant and unusual feature of the case, which was after all a case of capital murder, when everyone knew that the death sentence had already been repealed for most cases of murder, following upon public outrage over the execution of the notorious Ruth Ellis.

Next day saw the close of the case for the prosecution and I was not surprised to hear, from Tam Pearse's opening speech to the jury, that he did intend to call his medical evidence, and Dr Mary Hambly was an attractive young woman and a good witness, with a particular hobby horse which was that shell shock could be the cause of Isabel Earl's loss of speech. But the witnesses for the prosecution were very able as well. It would be for the jury to decide which set of medical opinions was right, although I had little doubt myself, of course I must not let that show in my final summing up to the jury on the facts which were of course in this as in any criminal case for them to decide. I had suffered myself from judges who went all out for a conviction and I must try my hardest not to do the same. Was the opinion of the presiding judge at a trial really of no significance at all? I asked myself. I knew that however much I told the jury that it was their opinion on guilt or innocence that counted, and only theirs, it would still be likely that they would want to know what I thought myself. It might not be decisive but it would be a factor for them. It would not be human for me not to form my own opinion, after the case had been going on before me for several days, and at the last resort the law did require me to have an opinion even if this were for one purpose only – if I thought that the case had not been proved, and that no jury could convict on the evidence before them, then in those circumstances it was my clear duty to withdraw the case from the jury and order them to find the defendant "not guilty".

And then we heard the final speeches of the two counsel in the case. Mervyn Griffith was logical, cool and devoid of emotion, which was all quite proper for counsel for the prosecution in any case. But he drove home the undoubted facts in a clinical way. Tam Pearse then made an excellent and moving speech for the defence. Just for a moment I began to wonder whether the prosecution really had been able to rule out any possibility other than that this had been a deliberate killing. I looked again at the silent figure in the dock. Isabel Earle had been unmoving during the entire trial. No flicker of emotion had ever crossed her face. But I remembered my own clear duty to ensure that the public were to be protected if possible. I began my own summing up of the evidence and my own directions to the jury on the law. It was nearly the end of the day and so I left just a little bit of my summing up for the next day. I explained the reason for this to the jury since otherwise it might have seemed a little odd that I had not finished the job when so little of it remained. If I had finished my summing up to them they would have had to retire at once to consider their verdict, in their own room or in a hotel. They would have had to have been kept separate from everyone who might have influenced them, even, or perhaps especially, their own families. They would have been kept under the watchful eyes of the Jury Bailiffs until they had reached a verdict, or decided that they were not going to be able to do so. As it was I could send the jury away for the night with the usual admonitions to talk to nobody about the case and be influenced by nothing they heard about it from the press or other media. The next day I concluded my summing up and waited in my room to be told, at last, not that the jury had reached a verdict as I was expecting but that the jury wanted to ask a question. The court had to reconvene and when everyone was once more in their proper place and I had entered with the usual flourish I read out the question from the note that had been handed to me as I had waited reading my paper in my room. It said:

"'We believe that the defendant is in need of medical treatment as recommended by Dr Hambly – but we cannot be certain that the fatal shot was fired on purpose rather than by accident – can the court make an Order that she now receives that treatment?"

"Mr Griffith-Jones, Mr Pearse," I said and both counsel dutifully rose to their feet.

"This can only mean that the jury are not sure that the charge of capital murder has been made out – if they cannot be certain that the shot was fired on purpose. I shall accordingly direct them to return a verdict of 'not guilty'."

I did so at once and noticed the relief which passed over the faces of each one of them. I looked at the defendant and saw that her own face was calm as ever. I noticed that Chief Inspector Hollingsworth was no longer in court but that the young DC Trevor Hughes had been left to look after things for the police. It seemed to be only a small gesture of human kindness to arrange for Isabel Earle to be accompanied back to her home by some of those still in court. Her friend Elsie Collins and Dr Mary Hambly both agreed to go with her and arrange for any medical treatment which might be necessary. There was also the young Detective Constable who had given evidence for the prosecution, who could organise transport for the small party going back to the defendant's old home in North London.

The result of the trial was not what I had expected. It was not what I had wanted. I had believed that the prosecution case had been made out and that the public at least deserved to be protected from any further madness on behalf of that dangerous young woman. But I had been obliged to discharge her without a stain upon her character. The jury had not been convinced that the prosecution had made out their case and that was an end of the matter. At least it was the end of the matter for Isabel Earle. I may have had my own doubts about the views of Dr Mary Hambly, but she had certainly seemed to be well qualified in her subject and I knew that it could be that she was right after all and that the experts for the prosecution had been wrong. In effect that was exactly what the decision of the jury had meant. The prosecution had no appeal from that verdict and it was certainly not for me to question it. My own concerns for the future of the lady continued, but at least I had done what I could to ensure that she should remain under good medical care. She would also be returned to the familiarity of her own home and would be surrounded by her friends. I hoped that the attractive young woman might soon find some other less violent protector than her former husband.

All the world's a stage,
And all the men and women merely players;
They have their exits and their entrances;
And one man in his time plays many parts...

W. Shakespeare

Chapter Six

Of course, a free and true confession to the offence with which an officer wishes to charge a criminal, is what every honest cop hopes for. The dangers and evils of the "verbal" or false confession, had been drummed into us all by the boss at Stoke Newington, DCI Hollingsworth. But what I am about to write is not a false confession but "the truth, the whole truth and nothing but the truth" just like the words on the card, which witnesses swear before giving evidence in a court of law. I certainly hope that the following account of it all never sees the light of day and is never opened by DCI Hollingsworth himself, to whom I am addressing it in the traditional sealed envelope inscribed: "Not to be opened until after my death." Dangerous? Well certainly that, but I shall be sure to hide it well and the saying that "Confession is good for the Soul" is a true one. I have a strange compulsion to do this. Perhaps it is caused by a long training in getting at the truth of things, I don't know, but I do know that my mind will be a lot easier once I have done it. And while I am about it I shall make it into the perfect confession – everything that happened as I see it, without any reservations at all.

When your father has been a policeman, and his father before him, then the choice of a career becomes a little bit easier. I liked what I had always seen of the Police Force; the friendships within it, the organised life of a police officer, the social life which embraces the whole of the policeman's family, provided only that they want to be part of it all. My father was a sergeant, stationed first of all in London and later on at Oxford. So after I had done my training I started life on the beat in Oxford. But it is not always too good to be under the parental eye, and anyway my ambition was to become a detective, for which exciting service there were no vacancies in the C.I.D. at Oxford. Becoming a plain-clothes officer is an ambition for a great many young coppers. Apart from the glamour, it is reckoned to be a lot more interesting for the intelligent young man anxious to make his mark in life. The hours are less rigid, the chances of distinction are greater. There is always the chance of being the one to assess the vital clues correctly and perhaps to make the right guess, which leads to the breakthrough and identification of the criminal in question.

At last in September 1960, I was delighted to hear that my application for a transfer had been approved, although it meant a move away from Oxford with its "dreaming spires" to the smog of London. Smog, because this was 1960 and the Clean Air legislation had not begun to bite. The pea-soup fogs still occurred, when you could hardly see your hand in front of your face. But there were compensations to be found in the more varied nightlife of the great metropolis. I settled quickly at Shoreditch Police Station and met my new colleagues. North London I discovered, had got its fair share of villains, but the cockney character was full of interest. I had to live down the nickname of "Professor Hughes" which was an obvious choice for my new friends. Had I perhaps acquired the slightest gloss of an Oxford accent? I didn't really think so, but it was not really a cockney accent whatever else it was, and I suppose that I stood out a bit from the others. In reality I was not so much a professor as the rawest kind of student, studying a different perspective of police work and in particular the criminal mind. I always remembered the words of some learned judge of the past who had said that: "…the state of a man's mind is as much a fact as the state of his digestion" and of course, for the police it was always necessary to establish the basic facts. One of the most important of which was the criminal's intention, very much a question of the state of his mind. I was thinking of this, when I and some four more of my colleagues were gathered together for a briefing in relation to an imminent raid on a house where it was suspected that firearms were secreted.

Detective Chief Inspector Hollingsworth came into the room and we all stood respectfully and sat down again to listen to the details of the raid we were about to make. We were going to look for an arms haul in a house in Clacton Street. The owner, Henry Earle, was suspected of having been behind a number of armed robberies which had taken place in North London over the past several months. Although we had sometimes been able to arrest the men who had taken part, we had never found any of them to be in possession of any firearms even if the victims were positive that they had been threatened with revolvers or pistols during the robbery. In particular, acting on a tip-off some weeks before, we had raided a house not far from Clacton Street, just after an audacious robbery of a jeweller's shop in the nearby High Street. We had been given the correct information and acted speedily. We had caught two known villains "bang to rights" with some of the stolen goods still hidden in their houses. We knew that the three robbers concerned had been armed since the jeweller had been threatened with pistols. He had even known something about guns, or had thought that he did, so that he had said to them:

"Go on, I know a fake when I see one."

But this was met with the immediate response that one of the men, all of whom had stockings pulled over their faces, had fired a shot into the floor. That had meant the end of any resistance, and they made a hurried collection of everything that they could take from the safe that he had opened for them, before leaping out of the front door and into the waiting car outside it. Although a good many of the stolen goods were recovered from the houses of two of the men we had been informed about, no firearms were found in either of them. In the case of the third man no stolen goods were found. So there was no evidence against him and he could not be arrested; much to our chagrin since we had been almost sure that he had been one of them. At the subsequent trial of the other two, there was little doubt of their guilt since each had been found in possession of his share of the stolen jewellery. Neither had been able to provide himself with any alibi or reasonable explanation as to how he came to be in possession of stolen jewellery. There were no signs of any firearms in either of their homes. The third man had also had his home searched from top to bottom but again nothing had been found. In his case there was no evidence of identification since all three men had been very effectively masked with stockings and all had been wearing nondescript clothing. The two who had been caught with stolen property in their homes had got no real defence to a charge of receiving stolen property knowing it to have been stolen and pleaded guilty at their trial. For lack of evidence we could not charge them with the more serious offence of being the actual robbers, and the third man, however clearly we thought we knew who he was, escaped altogether through lack of evidence. But if our informant had been right twice – then surely he would have made no mistake about the third man.

No sane copper would dream of putting his informer into the witness box to give evidence at a trial. For a start the informer would be likely to have a decidedly dodgy record himself and so would be open to cross-examination as to his own bad character, causing the jury to doubt that they could safely convict on his evidence. In any event it was likely to be "hearsay" evidence based on underworld gossip, and so inadmissible in a court of law. Most importantly, it would mean the end of the services to the police of that particular valuable source of information, since all his crooked friends would know exactly what he was. Convictions had been obtained against two robbers but only for the lesser offence, and the third had escaped altogether. Which was very frustrating after the excellent police work which had been done. The fact that no weapons had been found in the possession of either of the convicted men, and that no stolen property was found in the house of the third, probably meant that the third man had just been lucky and had managed to dispose of his share of the loot very quickly. The fact that no weapons had been found in any of the houses searched also almost certainly meant that there was a "Minder" at work in our district, so that the weapons used had been returned at once to him.

The informer had already identified the minder as Henry Earle of 12, Clacton Street, a man suspected of much, but against whom no crime had ever been proved. Detective Sergeant Bill Bernard had known his prize informant for years, but he would never say who he was. Nor how he got his information, or why it was that the informer was indebted to him, so much that he was prepared to risk life and limb by "grassing" on his pals for the meagre rewards that police funds could stand by way of payment for his services. It was part of the pact between them that the relationship was one to one; never shared; never disclosed. Even the boss, Detective Chief Inspector Hollingsworth did not know. A police station is after all, a closed circle and if any of us knew the man's identity, or could it possibly be a woman, then it would not be long before we all did and not much longer before the word got out outside our own "Nick". X had now given further information which caused us all to prepare for the raid on 12, Clacton Street which was to take place in the early hours of the following morning. The Governor went over the facts and apportioned the areas for our search. I was allotted to the back bedroom and reflected that it did not seem a very likely place to find an arms hoard.

At the unearthly hour of 5.30 am the following morning I found myself rushing through the front door of Henry Earle's house, which had been broken open by a couple of blows with a sledge hammer, wielded by Detective Sergeant Bill Bernard himself. The tousled half-clad figure of Henry Earle came running down the stairs, and he was taken to the kitchen by two of my fellow cops, in spite of his protests, which soon lapsed into a sullen silence. Earle was a dark, now silent figure who seemed to be bowing to the inevitable. Perhaps he had a clear conscience? Somehow I did not think so, but did not pause in my rush upstairs to the room I was to search. On opening the door of the back bedroom I thought at first that there was no one in it although I did see the rumpled double bed and the heap of bedclothes, and when I turned on the light I saw that someone was hiding under them. It looked very much as if the someone was a woman since I noticed women's clothing draped over the bedside chair.

"You must know we are the Police," I said to try to comfort the shrouded figure, "…just stay quiet, and no-one will hurt you. But I have a duty to do and that is to search this room, so I'll just have to get on with it."

There was no reply and I began my search. A likely place might be the dressing table and I began to go through the drawers, which revealed an assortment of lingerie and pieces of costume jewellery. They were mixed together indiscriminately and I lifted some out to see behind them in the drawer. I knew that the figure on the bed behind me must be that of Isabel Earle, the 27 year old wife of the suspect whose house we were searching. I happened to glance into the mirror in the dressing table in front of me and was fascinated to see a naked leg reach onto the floor beside the bed and then a woman surreptitiously slid out from under the bedclothes. She was decidedly pretty. And she was wearing only a T-shirt that did little to hide her attractive and very curvaceous young body. She now took off the T-shirt and stood demurely, startlingly naked before picking up a pair of pink panties that were draped over the chair in front of her. She glanced quickly towards my back and I pretended to be engrossed in my search but my eyes were riveted to the sight of Isabel Earle. She lifted one leg and stepped into her panties getting one buttock in and then after a slight pause the other; then she gave a firm wriggle to get the panties up to their proper place, fitting neatly but rather inadequately, round her very shapely bottom. There had been rumours at the Shoreditch nick that Henry Earle was "having it off", not with the lovely Isabel his wife, but one Irene Barret the wife of a man serving a long "stretch" in gaol, and I was wondering if these rumours could possibly be true, when I saw that Isabel was now standing looking at my back, her panties on her body but her bra still on the back of the chair.

"You're peeping," she said accusingly.

I could only turn round and now stare unashamedly at her as she picked up the bra.

"No, Oh No!... well maybe... it would be a sin not to... I couldn't really help it."

I stammered as the performance with the panties was repeated with the necessary variations in relation to the bra. Again the scanty garment seemed too small, or Isabel's breasts were on the large side; but I reflected that they were just as shapely as her sexy bottom.

"Shut your eyes," ordered Isabel.

"I'd really rather not... there are some sights that are really worth seeing... and all in the line of duty since I've been ordered to make a very thorough search of this room. I think that that means that I really ought to search you too?"

"You must be joking... .anyway you can see I've got nothing to hide..."

And so I told her what we knew about Henry Earle and the need to search her house. But I thought that Isabel was not a bit upset and seemed rather taken with the idea of a body search. If the rumours about Henry's affair with Irene Barret were right then could it just be that she might welcome something different herself? She did not seem to mind too much that she had had an audience. I even wondered whether all that sexy wriggling had been really essential for getting into them.

"So now I've got something on at least... where do you want to search?"

It was as close to an invitation as I was likely to get.

"Some prisoners hide stolen property inside their mouths," I said and I pulled her to me, gently at first but then with ardour. She made no resistance as I kissed her and this encouraged me to put my arms around her and my tongue inside her opening mouth and I did begin to make a very thorough search of it. But then there was a shout outside from Sergeant Bernard.

"Come on Trevor we haven't got all day... but do be thorough because there might be a lot of kit hidden there somewhere... we haven't found anything down here yet."

So I made a further hurried but very thorough search of Isabel's now responding body and its most secret places. I had never enjoyed police duty so much before and I comforted myself with the thought that now I could be really sure that Isabel was hiding nothing from me. And then with great reluctance, I had to put her down and finish my search of the room. It revealed nothing and Isabel protested loudly but without much conviction as I examined each of a collection of fancy undies. I noticed that her dressing had still not got further than the pants and bra stage and there were various other parts of her body that seemed to be crying out to be searched again. But I decided that I should have to join the others.

I caught her to me for a last moment. "A copper has to be sure when he's making a search," I whispered. "...but now I have to go... could I come back to night to finish the job, or would Henry be at home?"

"No, he'll be out with his girlfriend after six..."

Well the search party retired defeated and Detective Sergeant Bernard, whose informant had started it all, was particularly frustrated and vowed to find out what had gone wrong if he possibly could. But the general opinion was that his information had been correct at the time it was given. But that somehow, word of our intention to raid 12, Clacton Street had got out, so that Henry Earle had had time to clear his house of all the hidden armoury before the raid took place. If this were true, would the seductive Isabel know about it? I almost blurted out that I had got on rather well with her and would try to find out the answer. But luckily I decided to be more discrete. The thought that I could be combining duty with pleasure was an attractive one. If news of my planned return to the scene of the search, on pleasure bent after duty that day, should happen to be discovered, then I could surely say that it had all been in the line of duty? In any event my own guess was that Isabel was not completely in her husband's confidence. His affair with Irene Barret seemed to show as much. It seemed unlikely to me that Isabel would really be a party to Henry's devious doings as a minder. But my pulse raced as I mused on how I should set about finding out just how much Isabel did know.

And so at 6.30 that evening I clocked off duty at the Shoreditch Police Station and made my way home, via 12, Clacton Street. During the raid that morning I had gone in to the house by the back door accessible only through a secluded alley and past the dustbins. I repeated this. Only a cat seemed to notice my furtive approach. If any of the neighbours saw me, I could pose as a zealous cop still on the job. But luck was with me and no one appeared until I was almost at the door, when it suddenly opened and Isabel came out on her way to the dustbin with the day's rubbish in her hands. But she was now dressed in a fashionable pink mini-skirt and tight fitting blouse. Without saying a word she put down the rubbish and pulled me inside the house. A couple of hours later I was once more in the upstairs back bedroom. My plain-clothes suit was thrown carelessly on a chair. Isabel was where I had first seen her and was back in the same condition of voluptuous nudity.

"You know that silly bastard of a husband of mine seems to think that I know nothing about his having an affair with that awful Irene Barret."

"How do you?"

"For one thing a woman always knows when something is going on… the absences, the late hours… the fact that now he hardly ever wants to do it with me… coupled with the local gossip. My neighbour Elsie Collins is a very good friend and would never want to hurt me but she does get all the local gossip. She told me to watch out for Irene. And then the silly bastard left a note from her to him, arranging a meeting, in his trousers pocket. And I'm not silly am I? I had a look and found it. And then I found a necklace he'd bought her hidden in the back of his clothes drawer, and it was very pretty and must have cost a bomb, so was he going to give it to me? Well of course he never did and it was gone from his drawer. Also I've seen them together, when they didn't know I was there, in the Derby Arms. So I do know. And he doesn't seem to think I can put two and two together, and he doesn't seem to think I care about his being out most nights. And he certainly doesn't seem to think that I might be going to get a bit of my own back."

"But now you are."

And I gently stroked her neck and then lower down her back, and then very gently began to explore again some other places. But she did not stop me and began to do some exploring of her own.

"So this is what you policemen call a body search? And what do you think you've found?"

But by this time I had stopped my manual search and only gave a few satisfied moans until I whispered in her ear:

"I think I might have found the right spot now."

So that was the first night of many. I had crept out of the house, this time armed with a spare key to the back door, and made my way home undetected and very happy. My casual affairs of the past were already fading to make room for a wonderful and new feeling. What was it about Isabel? She was somehow mysterious at the same time as beautiful and, as I had just discovered, very sexy. She seemed happy to try anything once, and I became determined that she should try everything I had to offer time and again. And so it came about that a routine police search of a house in North London developed into the greatest affair of my life. We invented our own code for my visits. If Henry had announced that he was going to be late, we knew that it meant that he was going to be very late. Isabel would hang out some washing on her line as a sign for me on my way home. It seemed to work very well. But as the weeks passed we both realised more and more that it could not go on forever. Sooner or later Henry would find out. Or would he leave Isabel to take up permanent residence with Irene before he did find out? Isabel's own attitude to this possibility was curious. In fact her relationship with Henry altogether struck me as very odd. She still seemed to feel quite a lot for him in spite of everything. In spite of her growing affection for me, which I was sure was genuine. In spite of his explosive bouts of violent temper which resulted in bruises and, once a black eye. She would not accept that Henry could possibly leave her for "that slut Irene". She gave me the firm impression that if he ever really did, Isabel would be quite irrationally upset. Women were funny creatures I reflected. Even those as fascinating and intelligent as Isabel Earle. It all increased my growing feeling that something must be done but what?

I soon learned from police sources, that it was strongly suspected that Henry was back to his old tricks of lending out his armoury for reward. Was it too much to hope for, I wondered, that one day he might have a drunken accident with one of his own firearms? But it was probably more likely that one of my own colleagues might happen to notice me slipping into, or out of, the back door of Number 12 Clacton Street one night when I should have been on my way to or from duty. Or a curious neighbour might notice and start asking awkward questions. The dangers added to the excitement; but common sense told me that something would have to be done. One night as I was gently stroking Isabel's long auburn hair after a particularly passionate session I asked more seriously than I had ever done before:

"What did happen to the arms hoard? You must have known about it before our raid on your house?"

"Oh, yes. Of course I knew what Henry was up to, although he never discussed it with me. He even used to keep some of the "hardware" as he called it, under some old rugs in the attic. He didn't seem to care if I knew all about it or not, but I knew he had got knives and pistols and he knew that I knew. Then one day just before your raid, there was a knock on the back door and a man came and whispered something to him and he hurried upstairs, went into the attic and came down with a big heavy suitcase; he rushed out to the car and he was off. So when you chaps came to search our house the very next day, why I don't think that there was anything left for them to find because I think that it must all have been in that suitcase."

"Do you know who this man was?"

"No, I did see him for a moment but all I can say is that he did look a bit familiar, although I don't think that I actually knew him... he might have been one of your pals?"

"How was he dressed?"

"He was wearing ordinary clothes, quite smart, I don't know why I thought he might be a cop... there was something about him even if he was acting furtively. Perhaps it was his boots? I can't say, it was just a sort of impression."

"Well if there was a tip off, there might well have been a bent cop involved... or perhaps only a cleaner... who knows? Of course, a friend of Henry's. But that was weeks ago now."

"Yes, but he's brought them back, the armoury, or some at least..."

And Isabel jumped out of bed, walked over to her dressing table and rummaged among the undies to bring out a nasty looking gun which I recognised at once as a traditional Colt .45.

A thought suddenly occurred to me. A very wicked thought for an honest cop.

"When he's knocking you about... you never hit him back of course? I imagine that if you did it would only make him much worse and you wouldn't stand a chance. I've never spoken to him but I did have him pointed out to me by another cop and he looks like a big tough fellow?"

"No, I'd never dare."

"But the law says that you can use reasonable force to defend yourself, you know? That means that if anyone is defending themselves against someone who is much bigger and stronger than they are, then they can quite reasonably redress the odds a bit? That is that it would be OK to pick up some kind of weapon? A chair leg perhaps? It might be going it as bit strong to actually pick up one of his own guns and shoot him with it but, if he had really been knocking you about, as he obviously does, even if there had been the use of a gun a clever barrister might get you off with a sympathetic jury on a defence that you had used no more than reasonable force to defend yourself."

"But I could never use anything like this..." and Isabel picked up the Colt .45 and looked at it gingerly.

"You had better let me look at that," I said and took it from her.

"Do you realise that this is fully loaded?" I said. "The safety catch isn't even on and it is highly dangerous. I'll give you a quick lesson in how to use it. Because you really ought to know... just in case, you ever did have to really defend yourself. If perhaps he came at you armed with some other weapon. At least you should know how to render it safe by putting the safety catch on. And you should never ever put your finger round the trigger, like this, because that, of course is how you fire it..."

And so I gave Isabel a quick demonstration on the use of the revolver. I then, without thinking but as the result of some instinct, wiped the handle to remove any fingerprints, and put it back in the very back of the undies drawer.

"I don't think I could ever possibly use that weapon, however violently he was beating me. I would never get the chance of getting it out; I would be much too frightened that I might kill him. And then it would be murder and I should hang for sure, shouldn't I?"

"Well I must say that it would be very likely, because if you were to be found 'guilty of murder' there is no other sentence open to the judge to pass upon you. But of course, as I've just said you could plead 'not guilty' and run a defence of 'self defence' or you could say that the beating he was giving you justified the use of the gun so as to reduce the charge of murder to one of manslaughter – or there is one other possibility. Very rare. However I did have a case in my previous station at Oxford years ago, where a wife did knife her husband who was attacking her with a hammer. The effect of such a violent incident was so traumatic that it literally struck her dumb. The defence got a psychiatrist to say that this was something called hysterical aphonia. It was like the soldiers who got shell-shocked during the war. Apparently she might recover her powers of speech some day, nobody could say when. Anyhow it got her off altogether. She pleaded 'not guilty' to murder and she was acquitted, although personally I always had my doubts about it and thought she might have been faking it all. She had once been a medical student and I thought that she was too clever by half and was probably 'guilty as charged'."

Isabel looked very thoughtful as she said, "No, I could never do anything like that. Anyway I've got used to being knocked about. It is part of marriage to Henry Earle. And then he does some things that make you think it is all worth while..."

But she didn't say what, so I could only guess what they were... but somebody had certainly taught the lovely Isabel some very interesting things to do in bed which came as surprises even to me and I had thought I knew a thing or two before ever we had met. I was on "early turn" the next night, which meant that I was on duty from 6 pm to 2 am and so there would be no chance of a night with Isabel. If I were to call round at anything after midnight I might find that Henry was back in his own home. So we bid ourselves a reluctant farewell and I left 12, Clacton Street and made my way back to the Section House where I lived. As I went I reflected on the strange beings that are women. I remembered that the French poet Racine had said over 200 years ago, "Elle flotte, elle he'sitate; en un mot, elle est femme…" So now I was hopelessly in love with Isabel. I would have risked everything for her, even my police career. It seemed I had no chance of a permanent relationship, even marriage, because in spite of everything Isabel seemed to retain some strange but quite strong feelings for Henry. At least she would not leave him. Would it ever change, I wondered? Could there be something which would push her over the brink and make her part from him? Well, I thought, there just might be. My friends in the police made fun of me and my love of Shakespeare. Thinking of Isabel I remembered his sonnet "Shall I compare thee to a summer's day? Thou art more lovely and more temperate…" and I suddenly remembered those lines from Byron about "Alas the love of women, it is a lovely and an awful thing." I seemed to remember that that was followed by the stark thought that if it did go wrong then "life has no more to bring to them." I did hope that this would not apply to Isabel if ever her undoubted past and even possibly still remaining love for Henry really did come to an end. What would happen if, or should it be when, she finally realised that Henry's love for her had soured in favour of the wretched Irene Barret? If that happened, would she leave him at last and come to me? Or would she be so distraught that she made some attempt upon her own life? Or could she make some bitter attack on Irene in a paroxysm of grief and rage? It did look as if my turn would surely come, she simply could not go on loving the fellow; and it was amazing that she still seemed to feel anything for him. She was a young woman of impeccable character and I had never seen her lose her temper in any way, so it did not seem likely whatever happened, that her reaction would be violent. But she would need solace and comfort from someone so why not me? She also obviously found that having sex was a necessary part of life and it did not seem that she was getting much of that from Henry either.

The next day I came on duty late, knowing that I should not leave the station until the early hours of the next day. As midnight approached Sergeant Emerson, who was the only uniformed officer present and in charge of Shoreditch Station that night, said that he would leave me on my own for half an hour, while he nipped out for a coffee and a sandwich at the all-night café in the High Street. When he had been gone for a little time, I thought that it would be a good opportunity to have a look at the hoard of weapons that had been seized in a recent police operation on the same lines as our raid on 26, Horton Street, but this one had been very successful and all the weapons we had been told about had been found to be in that other house. They had not yet been properly listed. Towards the bottom of the pile I came across a Colt .45 revolver similar to the one I had been explaining to Isabel so recently, and idly I picked it up. It too was fully loaded but with the safety-catch on. I knew that the pistol should never have been allowed to stay loaded and, for that matter, that Sergeant Emerson should have been re-listing the recovered hoard of weapons rather than going out for his sandwich. When he came back he might even ask my help to do that very thing. But as it was, that identical Colt .45 exercised a strange interest for me and, as I heard Dick Emerson approaching the door, without any clear idea as to why I did it, I slipped the Colt into the ample pocket of my raincoat which was hanging up on the wall beside me.

Just after 2 am I left the station and made my way back towards my Section House. I could not resist making the minor diversion which led me past No 12 Clacton Street. That was the state I was in at the time. I knew that I could not see her but I still wanted to be near her, or see any signs of her in the darkened house. I even wanted to look at her bedroom window, even if it would be to torment myself with thought of what might be going on in the bed inside. As I approached I saw that, unlike all its neighbours, it was not in darkness at all; there were lights on both upstairs and down. I turned down the little side alley, which led to Isabel's back yard. And then, just as I opened the gate to the yard, all hell seemed to break loose from inside. There was a loud explosion which I recognised all too well as the report of a firearm, probably a revolver. Then with hardly a pause there was a second. My imagination raced. I rushed to the back door and used my key to open it. There were two more shots in loud succession. I did not know if this was Henry shooting at Isabel or, just possibly the other way about. But if the report did come from a revolver in Isabel's hand, wildly improbable as this seemed, then I suspected that my lesson in its use would not have been very effective. Isabel had never fired a single shot even on a practice range, let alone in anger. She was bound to be a rotten shot and the Colt .45, the "Cowboys' friend" was known to have a wild kick and likely to miss the target in any but an experienced hand, so it seemed likely that the shot came from some weapon held in some other more experienced hand and aimed at her.

Mine also was an experienced hand, and I pulled out the Colt that I had put into my own raincoat pocket, just as there were two further shots in rapid succession and I opened the kitchen door to see a wild scene. Henry was standing at the open front door. Someone must have flung it open to flee the house. Isabel was standing against the wall in the little hallway with blood pouring down her leg. Henry had the Colt .45 in his hand but did not turn to see who had opened the door from the kitchen. He raised the Colt in Isabel's direction, it seemed clear that he was about to shoot her, and at that range he could not miss if there were any shots left in it. I did not pause but lifted my own revolver and fired. Fired for real; there was no time for half measures. I aimed at his head without conscious thought and saw him lurch out of the house and collapse on the pavement with his own revolver still clutched in his hand.

So, now was the time for very quick thinking. I had just shot a man with a revolver, which I should not have had. Without any provocation. In the house of my lover where I had no right to be. I looked at Isabel but she stayed leaning against the wall still pouring blood. She was apparently quite unconscious of her situation. Her eyes were closed as they had been since I first saw her. She did not open them now. I remembered the case of hysterical shock causing amnesia, that I had been talking about to her only the day before. Coincidences abounded in real life and I remembered to stay cool and to think logically as my training had taught me. I quickly went over the events of the last few seconds and realised that I had heard six shots before my own intervention. And a Colt .45 only holds six shots. So the revolver that Henry had been holding must have been empty, whether he realised it or not. So I had shot a man who was effectively disarmed. But now I had fired a shot of my own so that the extensive forensic examination of the house, which was bound to follow all too soon, would surely reveal as much. And at the moment I was the only person in the house. The wail of the siren of an approaching police car emphasised that that state of affairs would not last for long. A quick look at Isabel showed that she had not looked up and still seemed traumatised. The bleeding from the wound in her leg was not serious and it would be looked at properly very soon so I made no attempt at amateur First Aid. Instead I made a very quick re-examination of the kitchen where the fight for the gun must have started.

I noted some bullet marks in the walls made by shots which had either missed or had gone through the bodies of one or other of the unlikely combatants. I saw a bright gash across the front of the old fashioned cooker, which must have been made by the flattened bullet on the floor just below. I quickly put that shining, spent, flattened bullet in my pocket. Now any count of expended bullets should reveal six, the total inside Henry's revolver to start with. To fire at Henry to protect his own wife from his armed attack on her, was I felt sure entirely justified. But the events would be bound to result in my standing trial for something. I might get away with manslaughter but even that would inevitably mean disgrace, and the end of my career in the police, at the very least. At the worst, remembering that my affair with Isabel might well be revealed if I were to be arrested and charged with the shooting of her husband and in her house, it might easily mean a charge of murder and conviction of that would inevitably mean that I should be hung. So I had to act very quickly indeed to clear away any clues leading to the undoubted fact that I was the one who had fired the shot that killed Henry Earle, and not Isabel at all. If she were to be arrested as seemed likely if I left no trace that I had been there, then at least she would have some defence. Glancing at her now I saw that she was still slumped against the wall apparently oblivious to everything that was going on around her.

And then I heard the sound of a police car squealing to a halt, the pounding of police boots on the pavement outside the front door, and I hurriedly put the Smith and Wesson revolver in the pocket of the issue raincoat that I was wearing. There was nowhere else that stood any chance as a hiding place and I knew only too well that my fingerprints would be sure to be found upon it. I took up the pose of the attentive, helpful police officer who has just arrived at the scene of a crime. I went to the unresisting Isabel, took a clean handkerchief from my pocket and held it firmly over the wound in her leg. Sergeant Bill Hollings and two other policemen in uniform, who had formed the Response Unit, came bursting into the house. I explained that I had just been passing by on my way home when I had heard a fusillade of shots coming from No 12, a house I knew well from the abortive raid we had made upon it some weeks before.

"The front door was flung open and this man came lurching out and fell to the ground with that revolver in his hand, Sergeant," I explained. "There was obviously nothing to be done for him so I left him just where he was and came in here where I have managed to be a bit of help to this young woman."

"We'd better do nothing until the boss arrives," said Sergeant Bernard. "I sent for him as soon as I got the phone call from one of the neighbours explaining that they had been woken up by shooting coming from this house, and of course, I've sent for the Scene of Crime Squad."

And at that moment the Scene of Crime Squad arrived to be followed soon after by my own boss from Shoreditch, Detective Chief Inspector Hollingsworth, who seemed pleased to see me there.

"Trevor, I thought you were off-duty," he said, "...but as you are here, and as you know the house, you had better search the same part that you did before. I leave it to you what you look for, but keep an eye open for any other weapons that may have mysteriously reappeared. Or for that matter any documents. We don't know what happened here yet, let alone what caused it to happen. But you know the gossip is that Henry Earle was having an affair with Irene Barret. Possibly that could explain it all, there could be a bundle of love letters. You know what women are. They keep these things. Anyway see what you can find."

So off I went, remembering clearly the last time I had searched that bedroom some months before. I heard Mr Hollingsworth giving orders for some of the squad to question the neighbours, even if it was the middle of the night, and others to call the doctor and the ambulance, while he himself went out to the body lying on the pavement, leaving a young WPC to stand beside the silent Isabel to try to comfort her. Of course my greatest worry was that Isabel should come to her senses and seeing me, blurt out a greeting, or say anything else which would indicate our relationship and give the game away. But she still stood quite silent and seemed to be in some other world, far from Clacton Street. Just for a moment I wondered if after all she had remembered our recent conversation about hysterical aphonia, and was acting out that fantasy, but I dismissed the idea at once. Isabel was far too innocent to have planned all this... Anyway I must be busy and take advantage of the wonderful opportunity that had been offered to me. I hurried upstairs and searched the bedroom as carefully as I possibly could. I was searching for letters as instructed. But my prime object was to see if there were any letters, not from Irene Barret to Henry Earle, but from me to Isabel. Yes, I had written a few notes to her from time to time to arrange meetings. Loving words had certainly crept in. I knew that Hollingsworth was right when he said that women sometimes kept these things, reckless as that might be. But I found nothing and was reasonably satisfied that this was because there was nothing to find.

After that there was really little for me to do. But I had been very conscious of the Colt .45, in my raincoat pocket creating a considerable bulge, which might be noticeable to the others once the first excitement had worn off. Luckily my search for incriminating letters had revealed a reel of Elastoplast, and I managed to drop my trousers and tape the gun to the top of my inside leg. It was very uncomfortable, but it did the trick. So I waited upstairs as long as I decently could since this was away from Isabel and therefore the safest place for me. After all I had been told to make a thorough search. Then I reported back to DCI Hollingsworth. I found that he had organised the others to question the neighbours and that Henry Earle's body had already been taken away. There was no sign of Isabel herself who must have been taken away very quickly. So I would just have to hope and pray that she said nothing to implicate me and that she would escape any charge herself. After all, I comforted myself, there can have been no witnesses. Henry was dead and Isabel would just have to be very sharp witted. Or perhaps stay silent as she had been doing, because I knew that this could be a real case of "shell shock" of the kind I had described to her. It had happened within my own experience and what had happened once could happen twice. The circumstances were much the same. Or, could she possibly be faking, remembering what I had told her of my previous case? There was one thing that was certain and that was that I should not be able to ask her. Not now when she was in police custody. Perhaps never.

"Well, I didn't really expect you to find anything Trevor," said Hollingsworth, "...but you have to be certain in this game. It was lucky that you were passing and heard the shots so that you were the very first one here. I shan't forget your keenness; and I shall want a full report in writing in the morning of what you've already told me. But now you'd better get off home and get some sleep. You must be all in."

And so I took the chance and escaped. By the time I got to bed it was after 4 in the morning and I knew that I might be facing a squad from my own station, waking me up and arresting me at any time. Isabel could give the game away inadvertently in a hundred different ways; or perhaps even on purpose. I set my alarm for midday, knowing that I was due back on duty at Shoreditch at 6 pm and knowing that now there was nothing more that I could do to save Isabel, from the results of her own amazing and unexpected actions – or for that matter – to save my own skin from the results of actually killing the man.

When my alarm went off I lay in bed for a few minutes, turning it all over in my mind. I had picked up quite a good working knowledge of the criminal law after more than 10 years in the police. As far as Isabel was concerned there could be a good defence to any charge of homicide. This was that the only violence used was in self-defence. But violence, which resulted in killing a man, would need a situation of an extreme peril to begin to amount to justification. And of course, none of that could apply to me, however much it might have applied to Isabel, because she was being attacked and so might defend herself. I could not for a moment say that I had been under attack. So did the law allow one to kill a man in defence of someone else? I was not at all sure, although I was inclined to think that it might amount to sufficient justification to reduce any charge to one of manslaughter rather than murder. I knew that I should not be able to consult any lawyer to find out the answer; that would be far too dangerous. So the result was that I should just have to sweat it out. The enigma was Isabel herself – had she acted herself in self-defence? Or just given way to a wild outburst of temper when Henry had told her he was going to leave her. In spite of everything, was she still in love with him and not with me?... Or was it possible that she had remembered the case I had told her about, of that other young wife who, years ago, had escaped the hangman after knifing her husband because she had been struck dumb? I did not have the answer to any of these questions. I should just have to wait and see.

When I got back to Shoreditch at 6 pm I caught up with all the news from Detective Sergeant Bill Bernard, one of the team, the night before. There was no way I could get to see Isabel herself without arousing suspicion, but I could hear all about it at secondhand and so got to know, that she was keeping silent and that the doctors had been called in. It was natural that I should be interested in the case since I had been involved in it from the very start. I was off-duty for the next two days but when next in the office I read the psychiatrists' reports. Firstly I read two from very experienced consultants called in by the Director of Public Prosecutions. Their opinion was clear Isabel was insane. But she had been very far from insane in my judgement, and my work as a police officer meant that I had come across quite a few examples of those who really were. Could her awful experiences really have driven her crazy after just one night? I did not think so. The other possibilities were that she had remembered our conversations, had wanted Henry out of the way as much as I had, had done it deliberately and was now faking being dumb remembering the case I had told her about. But I remembered her horror at the mere suggestion that she might use violence in self-defence to an attack by Henry. And then I read the report of Doctor Mary Hamblin about her experiences with cases of shell shock and the effect that it sometimes had. From my own very personal knowledge of Isabel I thought that it could well be that Dr Hamblin was in the right.

I could only wonder. There was no way that I could speak to Isabel. I knew the defence team and the Solicitors, Purvis and Jarrold and I had met their Court Clerk Mr Hawkins. But I was a policeman, one of the "other side", even so I managed to meet Hawkins in his local pub one day and mellowed by a few drinks he gave a pretty full picture of the way he saw the case and the way that the defence was likely to be conducted by Tam Pearse the barrister he had briefed. I had played some part in all the events and had been the very first to arrive at the scene of the crime, so I was a witness and managed to make myself helpful and was able to attend the trial. I had a very nasty moment when the prosecution called a forensic expert to give evidence as to the bullet found in Henry's brain; the one which had killed him. This like the other bullets found in his body, had clearly come from a Smith and Wesson .45 revolver. He had no doubt about that at all. The markings on the bullet in his brain were however slightly different. I had a very nasty moment indeed as he said this, but he went on quickly to say that the difference was very slight indeed and could be accounted for in a number of ways, principally and most likely because this bullet unlike the others, had actually penetrated his skull which might possibly account for it. I heaved a sigh of relief when the expert said that he had discussed the whole point with the officers in the case and that the end result, since there was no suggestion that any other weapon had been used, was that they were from the same weapon.

I relaxed and sat quite still in my seat allowing my pulse rate to return to normal. Everything would still be all right. Throughout the whole trial Isabel sat in the dock, beautiful, remote. Our eyes rarely met and when they did she gave no sign of recognition. She was either still traumatised by the wild events of 21st March or she had remembered what I had said to her and was giving the performance of an accomplished actress, or could it possibly even be, a little bit of both?

I heard the defence put forward the possibility that Henry's death had been accidental. Although I found it hard to believe, I could see that in the absence of any witness, it was difficult to exclude it. And all the time of course, whatever my fears for Isabel and whatever my horror that my own part in it might come out, I had to pretend to be a dutiful police officer whose only concern was to ensure that justice was done. At last I was over the moon when I heard the verdict and had to fight hard to keep a sober face with just the hint of the disappointment that I should have been feeling. So the jury could not after all exclude the possibility that it had all been an accident. It was not the first time that I had been surprised in this way. I knew that juries could be unpredictable. What did it mean for me? Well of course it meant that Isabel was out of all danger whatever happened and whatever new evidence might come to light. At that time in 1961 it was the rule of the law that the same person could never be tried twice for the same offence. It did also mean that I was out of danger myself. A jury had decided that it had all been, or at least that it might all have been, nothing but an accident and one between Isabel and Henry alone. Then the judge, before discharging the defendant, turned to Tam Pearse the leader of the defence team, and suggested that his client should be taken home and receive whatever treatment Dr Hambly should recommend.

Humanitarianism is not always very obviously to be found in criminal courts but I think that everyone had felt some pangs of pity for the frail, beautiful young woman in the dock, and now everyone felt relief that the awful possibility of a death sentence was over. I was delighted to agree with the judge's suggestion that I see that Isabel and Dr Hambly had transport to get them back to Clacton Street. At last I should have the chance to speak to Isabel again. But in the event the nosy Elsie Collins somehow got included in the party and I could not very well stay behind on my own with Isabel. So Dr Hambly went off to the bedroom for a last private word with Isabel leaving me, luckily for only a short time, with Elsie Collins. As I waited I heard a newsvendor passing by and shouting the news story of the hour: "Isabel Earle acquitted. Will she be the last woman in peril of hanging? Read all about it." *The Evening News* was making a very big thing about it all and no doubt it would be the headlines in the dailies next day.

My wait was difficult since Mrs Collins wanted to talk it all over while I was in a fever to know the best, or the worst. Then Dr Hambly came back followed by an Isabel, still looking rather shocked. However she did seem to follow perfectly clearly what Dr Hambly was saying about taking sleeping pills, going to bed early and getting a good night's rest. There was no way I could have any private conversation with Isabel, and I was forced to stay silent. Elsie Collins promised to come back later with a "nice fish supper" and I could at least hold the front door open for the two ladies and be the last to leave. As I did so I looked straight into Isabel's lovely eyes of that deep Mediterranean blue and with relief, heard her whisper "I love you". And then just as Elsie Collins and I reached the street she called after us "Don't bother with the fish supper Elsie – I don't feel like anything but bed." Later that evening when I came off duty I hurried back to 12, Clacton Street. I went round to the back and used my key to get in for a tearful and passionate re-union.

Our affair went on almost as it had been before. Isabel did not want to talk about the events of the fateful day. Discretion had to be complete and that was not easy in a district like Stoke Newington and with neighbours who included Elsie Collins. We knew that this situation, in this neighbourhood, could not last. The only way we could go on would be to move to a new district as far away as possible from Clacton Street and start a new life. It was a stroke of luck that a distant cousin of Isabel's, her only known relation, was emigrating to Canada and had a very nice house to dispose of in Richmond. This was not nearly as far away as prudence dictated, but we reasoned that Greater London is a vast place, and that in practical terms it might well be just as effective as if we had emigrated to Canada instead of Cousin Cecilia. It was a difficult decision for me, because I had enjoyed life in the police. But I should have to resign and find some other way of earning a living. I also realised that it was not very appropriate for me to remain in a roll hunting criminals, when I knew perfectly well that I had become one myself, whatever justification I might find for what I had done. So I started making enquiries about a new job in Richmond, as a preliminary to handing in my resignation. I was lucky to find that the well-known and much respected local firm of solicitors, Ward Davey and Lewis, with offices in a lovely Georgian building facing Richmond Green, had a vacancy for a litigation clerk.

My exemplary service in the police was a good recommendation for the job. My only problem was that Isabel and I had decided that we needed to make a clean break from the past, which meant a change of names. In a curiously lovable way Isabel had always made it clear that living with her meant also, being married to her, and we had already decided that we should become Mr and Mrs Trevor Williams upon marriage. I explained some of this to the senior partner of Ward Davey at my interview. I added the slight fabrication that a favourite aunt had said she would advance me the money to buy a house on my forthcoming marriage and perhaps later leave me all she had, if I would only change my name to hers, which was Williams.

The reality was that the money for the purchase of the house was coming from the deceased man, Henry Earle himself. Isabel had explained that on the day before the police raid on her house, and our own first meeting, Henry had told her that he needed the house to himself for half an hour and she had dutifully gone next door to chat to Elsie Collins. When she came back she noticed that the house appeared unusually tidy – and that also unusually the tool shed in the garden had had its door unlocked. She explained that this was very unusual as the tool shed was sacred to Henry. She was not allowed inside it. She had always wondered why he seemed to regard it as so personal a place since he rarely did any gardening anyway. Of course Isabel had heard all the rumours about the way that Henry made his money and had never accepted his own explanation which was that his only source of money was from what he made as a "bookies' runner". He did in fact follow this other almost equally precarious occupation acting as the man who took the bets in the street in the 1960s, when street betting was strictly illegal, but was a universal and a lucrative way of making money. Had there been a store of weapons secreted in the garden shed all the time? After Isabel's acquittal we had made a thorough search of the house to ensure that no firearm had remained undetected in the various police searches there had subsequently been and we had found not a single one, and we had found nothing else of any significance at that time.

Now we did, as at the bottom of a locked toolbox, at the back of the same shed, we suddenly came across a large bundle of used £5 notes. Well Henry would not be able to use them, and it did not seem right to hand them over to the police. Much safer and much more useful, to keep them. Amazingly, they had amounted to just a little more than Cousin Cecilia was asking for No 3 Riverside View, Richmond. There seemed to be just a hint of poetic justice in the idea that Henry, having been such an indifferent husband, was now, indirectly and unknowingly, making amends by providing us with the means to start our new life together in comfort. And our life in Richmond went wonderfully well. It was like opening a new book. My parting from the police at Stoke Newington was accomplished with expressions of mutual regret. I had explained the family necessity which required it, and this was accepted without question. The marriage took place very quietly. The only witnesses were Cousin Cecilia, just before her departure for

Canada, and a stranger brought in from the street outside the Registry Office. No 3 Riverside View was furnished with the last of Henry's ill-gotten gains, and our new life started, and remained very happy for the next four years.

The only unfinished business that remained from my service with Stoke Newington CID was the Colt .45 Revolver that I had filched from them on the night of Henry Earl's death. I knew that I could not possibly return it to the rest of the confiscated armoury of weapons at the police station. It would be far too dangerous since it was just possible that some efficient officer might have it tested and find that it had been used or even that it too, matched the characteristics of the gun which had killed Henry Earl. So I had to "lose" it, first by hiding it in my own clothes cupboard in the Section House and later in my locked tool chest, which I took to the new house at Riverside View. Of course there was a fuss about the missing weapon, but because of all the excitement after Henry's murder, the loss was not discovered for several days. There were other Colt .45's in the collection and at last DCI Hollingsworth decided that there must have been a miscount of them, and the matter mercifully was shelved. So everything was very happy for me and Isabel; together at last.

And so it remained for the next several years until Ward, Davey and Lewis took on that ravishing young Articled Clerk, Katy Burnley. I have always been rather a restless sort of fellow and perhaps I had already been growing just a little bit tired of suburban bliss. Just a bit in need of a change from the compliant Isabel. Katy Burnley is a very young and very pretty blonde with long curly hair and a great figure. She has had a good education and is sure to pass her Solicitor's Exams and will probably get a partnership at Ward, Davey and Lewis. She has certainly been making a great play for me. I did not think that I was very much like Oscar Wilde and certainly not in his sexual orientation, but like him I have too often found that I could resist anything except temptation. It will be very hard for me to tell Isabel that I am leaving her after all we have been through together. But I shall have to do it. I think that she may already be getting just a bit suspicious of my frequent late nights "on duty". She has been looking at me rather strangely sometimes. Our own lovemaking of late has been not quite so rapturous, not quite so hectic and not quite so frequent. I know that the fault is mine and my thoughts have been elsewhere. So I think I'll tell her this evening. Keeping up this journal, recording everything about my affair with Isabel Earle, now Isabel Williams, has always been the most suicidal thing to do; it is against all my instincts. To keep it in an envelope addressed to DCI Hollingsworth is also quite mad. Some strange compulsion makes me do it and of course no one could ever possibly find it. Of course no one ever will since I keep it securely locked in the one drawer of my desk at Ward, Davey and Lewis to which only I have a key. When I have split with Isabel and gone off with Katy Burnley, I shall certainly destroy it, probably tomorrow?

'tis strange... but true; for truth is always strange;
Stranger than fiction.

Lord Byron, Don Juan

Chapter Seven

Well, of course I really knew that Henry was leading a life of crime. He never said so and I did not ask about it because I preferred to pretend, even to myself that it was not true but I knew that it was, without the need for the many hints I received from Elsie Collins and others. Of course I suspected what it was all about, even though we never talked about it. Perhaps I should have tried to, because I knew that it could not go on forever. I had heard the rumours and thought that it was only a question of time before the law caught up with him. But to start with at least, I did love the guy. He was fantastic in bed, even if he did get too rough at times I did not really object. Even if it was a bit dodgy to be a bookies' runner, as he said that he was, whatever he was really doing seemed to pay off very well and we were leading a very comfortable life. So yes, I knew that the bookies' runner was only a pose. But he did sometimes go out on street corners leaning against the wall, taking bets for George Osborne turf accountant, down in Thurvill Street. I suspected that the cash back he got from George was not the only reason that he did it. It certainly provided him with some money but it also meant that he was available to meet his real clients the thugs and robbers of the underworld. I also knew all about the very dubious types who would come to the front door, or sometimes the back. Henry never talked about them and would say that they had only come to place a bet. That might sometimes even have been true. Quite what else was going on I was never sure about. I did not really want to know, why should I? I certainly could not put a stop to it whatever I thought myself. I did however form an idea that Henry was keeping firearms for his friends, to be lent out at a high price when there was some nasty armed robbery in the offing, although I never actually saw any or knew where he kept them; I did not want to.

Elsie Collins was quite specific that he was a minder and explained to me exactly what that was. But I was still not certain, and it did not seem to matter all that much. After all, we were married and that meant a lot to me, brought up as I had been as a church going girl, as I still was. And of course a loyal wife had to support her husband and believe in him in all things. So it might have gone on for much longer. Then the rat started to pay attention to that slut Irene Barret. I did not need Elsie Collins to tell me that something was going on with another woman, but she did help to fill in the details. I realised later that Henry must have just managed to clear all his illegal hardware out before the police raid; he always kept the garden shed tightly locked and I suspected that that was where they must have been hidden and that was something I never knew for sure, but in view of later events the garden shed seemed most likely. The raid itself was a complete surprise to me, in more ways than one. First I had no idea that it was going to happen. To begin with I did not connect it with his surprise request a few days before it happened that I should go to the pictures with Elsie Collins, at his expense, which of course had given him a clear run to move the weapons' hoard to some other even safer place. Local gossip had let me down for once, and of course Henry himself said not a word.

It had been a shock when there was a banging on the door in the middle of a night when, for once we were both in bed together and I at least was fast asleep. When Henry jumped out of bed with a curse and rushed out of the room pulling on his clothes as he went, I just snuggled down and hoped that it would all go away without bothering me. It was not so easy to even make pretence of being asleep because then I heard men in the house and a lot of shouting so I pulled the bedclothes over my head and pretended not to be there. Then the door opened and someone came in. Peeping out I saw that it was a man in ordinary clothes, but I suspected that he was a plain-clothes policeman. He paid no attention to me but started to search the room and went at once to my dressing table pulling the drawers open. I peeped out and could see a man with his back to me. I saw that he was young and good-looking. Very good-looking, I decided as he turned his head and looked at the shrouded body in the bed which was me. I did not wear very much in bed. OK then, to be exact I did not wear anything at all, except a t-shirt. So what could a girl do when there was a good-looking stranger in the room and she was stark naked under the cover of the bedclothes?

Well he seemed to be pretty engrossed in searching my drawers and my own clothes were close at hand, just on the back of a chair beside the bed. So I nipped out and hurriedly started to put on my panties. They were certainly on the small side, as Henry had used to like, when he had noticed such things. They were rather tight as he had also liked, in the days when our love was young and passionate. They were pink and lacy with very pretty roses at strategic places. Yes, I admit that I had a bit of a struggle to get them on as Trevor later told me with graphic

215

detail. At the time I had my back to him but heard the sound of his rummaging in my drawers suddenly stop and turned round to see him staring at me with frank appreciation. When we talked it over later I discovered that his memory of our conversation that day was rather different from mine which was that he said:

"What a lovely rump."

"Thank you for nothing... I don't know who you are and I don't want your opinion... and it is not a rump. I'm not a horse... .I think you must mean my bottom... and please get on with your work and stop staring at me or I shall call the Police."

"I am the Police."

"Do stop peeping and let me get some clothes on."

Reluctantly he turned to continue his search.

"And promise not to peep," I said sternly. But the truth was that I was more than a little pleased to have the proof that I could still attract male admiration after a long gap when my own husband's attention seemed to have wandered elsewhere. I turned round again and struggled into my bra. A glance in the wall mirror showed me that the young cop had now quite abandoned his search of my dressing table and was staring at me with unconcealed lust. But I was amazed when he said out of the blue:

"Did you know that your husband was seeing another woman?"

"Well, I have heard rumours but I don't believe everything I hear – and how on earth do you know?"

"Well, we do know quite a bit about Henry Earle now."

"Maybe, but how do you know that?"

"You must realise that we don't make a raid like this, at this time of day, without making all sorts of enquiries first. Anyway the other woman is well known to the police because her husband is a bad lad too. His name's Barret and we strongly suspect that he was one of Henry's customers and had one of his guns on his person when we caught him in the act of the armed robbery of an elderly couple. Since we caught him in the act, it was of course before he had had the chance to hand the gun back to Henry. We never managed to prove that Henry was involved, because the old criminal code came in, and Barret just clammed up and wouldn't say a word. He went down for seven years and he still has quite a bit of it to serve. So his wife Irene is up for grabs for the likes of Henry… only this time our information is that it is all getting a bit serious and they've fallen in love with each other. Who is to say? Now don't tell me that you don't know anything about all this? That you haven't noticed anything?"

"Well, I have begun to wonder and my friend Elsie Collins, knows almost everything that's going on round here, and she was talking to me about this same woman, only yesterday. Irene Barret I know well, cheap little trollop; I never liked her."

"She is a very pretty woman."

"She is a tramp; nothing but a slut and well known for it, even before her husband got put inside. I suppose she must have got something that I can't see, because I know she has always been popular with the blokes."

"It's an insult because you are in a different class... but suppose... just suppose, that I had taken quite a fancy to you myself? Because we haven't got much time to talk... I'm supposed to be doing a job, and I ought to get on with it."

"Well why don't you?"

"Well, never mind that... but we haven't got much time... would you come out with me for a meal or a drink one night? Maybe get a bit of your own back? Maybe it would turn out to be something rather special... what do you think?"

"Well, there would be all sorts of difficulties for me. Perhaps for both of us. The word would get around. Very soon too, if we were spotted in any of the local pubs..."

His face fell. He was very good looking; clean looking too. So after a pause I went on; and then the die was cast.

"...but you could always come round here one night if you wanted to. And bring a bottle of wine and some fish and chips... or I could knock you up an omelette or something simple?"

"When shall we say?"

But before I could answer he had taken me very firmly in his arms and was kissing me with skill and passion – lots of passion. His arms went round me and I was still only in my panties and bra. And his hands were everywhere. Everywhere they should not have been, and it was getting exciting. I was getting very aroused indeed. Sex with Henry had been non-existent of late, and it was a long time since I had experienced lovemaking from anyone else, let alone anyone as good looking and virile as this young policeman whose name I did not even know. Anyway, disgraceful as it was I found that I could show no resistance whatsoever. He could have had me then and there. But I had no time to despise myself, because just at the point of no return, I heard a voice shouting up from downstairs:

"Have you finished yet Trevor... have you found anything? If so it will be the only things we have found... amazingly the place seems to be clean. Come down as soon as you can and report."

"I can now report I have not found a thing..."

Trevor shouted, just at the moment when I thought that he had found something rather important.

"...OK, Sarge, I've almost finished and have nothing to report..." and then into my ear "...when can I come round then?"

"As it happens I know that he is out tonight... he told me not to bother with supper for him. He will be with Irene I suppose... he is bound to be back here but much later than midnight. He always is nowadays. Would that suit you?"

"It certainly would."

"Then I'll hang out my panties and bras on the clothesline at the back where I think you must have come in… if the coast is clear. Probably that will be just after 6.30 when he goes out. You know the house now and you can get round the back through the alleyway if all is well. You will know that it will be if you see my undies… that is if you are sure you really want to…?"

"Yes, I do really want to… I'll see you tonight then… and the next night, and the one after that or whenever…"

Then he was gone and Henry did go out and Trevor did come round with a bottle of wine and some fish and chips. We found that what had started as a police search went on as a very passionate encounter that went on to a wonderful affair. Henry was out most nights. Trevor came round most nights. He became a habit and then he became very much of a part of my own life. Can a girl be in love with two men at once? I think that the books and everything that I've talked about with my friends, say that that is not possible. Yet in my case it seemed that it was. Although I was betraying Henry, Henry had started by betraying me. Yet he had been the first love of my life and although I really had no doubt about this now, I still could hardly believe it, I still did not want to. It was so humiliating to be supplanted by Irene Barret of all people. So that I really was leading a double life, but now I was having a wonderful sex life. Which of these two men in my life would turn out to be for real, and which would fade away into a thing of the past? For Trevor there was no doubt and he planned for our future and gradually I found myself taking a part in that instead of denying it was possible. When our affair had been going on for several weeks I told him about my guess that Henry had had a tip-off and removed all the weapons, just before the police raid which altered my life. I remembered that I was pretty sure that Henry had already brought some back. There had been renewed knocks at the door late at night, more furtive comings and goings to our house and I knew that one weapon was back again in my own bedroom and so I jumped out of bed and showed it to Trevor.

He said that it was a Colt .45 revolver and that it was dangerous because it was fully loaded and he showed me how to fire it. He also told me all about the defence that a crime had been committed only in self-defence. I knew perfectly well that he was suggesting that for him the perfect solution to it all would be that I should shoot Henry "in self-defence" when he was beating me up, and that I could get off a charge of murder for that reason. I did not suppose that he really meant it, he was just putting out a theory that would solve all his problems, and I knew perfectly well that I could never do any such awful thing. In a funny way although one part of me knew it was true about Irene Barret, another part still could not quite believe that Henry was doing it to me. I could not quite believe it when Trevor told me that his information was that Henry was going to tell me he was leaving me that very night. After he had gone I felt the same. It could not really be true. I knew that Trevor would not be round because he was on duty that night, so I just went to bed but I could not get to sleep. Then I heard Henry coming in and it was early by his standards. He did not come into the bedroom to start with but I could hear him moving about the house. Then I heard a noise that could have been Henry pulling out our large suitcase from under the stairs; and then the door opened and he was in the room. I pulled the bedclothes over my head as he turned on the light. Then he said:

"Now don't pretend to be asleep Isabel. I know you're not…"

So I sat up in bed and there he was standing in his smart "going out to visit Irene" clothes. He had the suitcase in his hand. So it was true after all. I got out of bed to hear him say:

"…you must have heard the rumours, about me and Irene Barret, They are true and I've fallen in love with the girl in a way I never did with you – with all your puritan principles. And 'no sex on Sundays'. Now I've only got to clear out my clothes from this room and I'm off…"

He started to open his shirt drawer while I lay in bed as the realisation really dawned on me. Well I never thought I had a temper or that I did things on the spur of the moment, that wasn't me at all. But somehow his actually saying it, made me go berserk. I didn't think. I just leapt out of bed rushed to my dressing table, opened the drawer, took out the Colt .45 pushed off the safety catch and I shot the bastard. This one did not kill him, I think it must have hit his shoulder, but it was enough to make him rush out of the room and I ran after him still shooting. In the hall, he got hold of me and got hold of the gun, but I managed to hold onto it. Then there was a struggle just by the front door. And then the gun went off again and I felt a great pain in my leg and then I realised that I no longer had the gun in my hand. Henry had managed to get hold of it himself; I think I was becoming traumatised but in a haze I realised that he had opened the front door, or that it had burst open anyway, and he was going out. Then I did black out. Just as I was losing consciousness I thought that I heard another shot but everything was very hazy, and then everything went black. The psychiatrists told me later that it was not uncommon for a very great shock to produce this effect. Anyway for me it did and everything went to a merciful blackness. Nothing mattered anymore, what a merciful relief it was. It seemed to last for hours. Then much later it seemed, I did come round; I was still standing up but slouched against the wall in the hall when I began to realise what I had done. I saw several policemen in uniform in the house. Then there was a woman cop standing beside me mopping my face with a wet flannel from the bathroom. Thank God, I had a few minutes to think while I apparently came to my senses, and while she was mopping my face with my flannel from the bathroom which she must have soaked in cold water while she kept saying soothing things.

So I had done it after all. When it came to it I really had shot Henry although I had told Trevor that I never possibly could. I had really meant it and believed that I could never possibly do any such awful thing. So what had happened to me when Henry blurted out that he was leaving me? I should have been delighted because of course it meant that I could go off with Trevor who I had begun to think very strongly was the man that was really meant for me. So why had I done it, committed murder most foul, when it gave me a happy release and when after all, I was still a bit in love with the bastard? I had a long, long time to think about this question, but I never really arrived at any answer. "Frailty thy name is woman" I remembered some poet had said sometime; but had anyone ever said: "Impetuous, unpredictable, unreasoning, perverse – that is a woman." I should have to ask Trevor, who knew a lot of poetry and was always quoting it to me. Somehow I did not think there was anything in poetry which mirrored the situation. In the cold light of reflection that was now upon me it did seem that this was the way I had behaved, but then I had not been thinking rationally, I had really had no time to think at all; I just acted on blind instinct born out of the crass stupidity of the man I had married and done so much for, in spite of the fact that I really knew how much of a crook he had always been. Perhaps that man Freud would have known the answer.

Then, I suddenly heard one policeman tell another that the doctor had said that Henry was quite dead with a bullet through his brain. So it was confirmed that I really had killed him; and now as my senses really came back to me, I remembered everything that Trevor had said. That I would hang. I remembered also about the case he had had of the woman accused of murder who had been so shocked that she could not speak, or said she could not, and she'd got off; at least she had not hanged. That must be my only chance now, and not much of one at that because I had never been much of an actress at school. Too transparent they had said; well I must not be transparent now. It seemed to be my only chance. After all they could not expect me to be faking when they would not know that I'd ever even heard of that other case; or had ever heard of shell shock in the war for that matter. So I said nothing. Nothing to any of the police who questioned me. Nothing to the doctors who examined me, both then and later. Nothing even to the solicitors who were instructed on my behalf.

Do not think that it was easy but I knew that my life depended on it. All I had to do was keep silent. You might be surprised at how difficult that is. When someone just asks you if you'd like a cup of tea – and you instinctively want to say "Yes, I'd love one", well you just have to school yourself to nod or shake your head and after a time of course, you do get used to doing that. As long as you remember that you will surely be hanged if you ever forget – well then you don't forget and it did make life easy for me. I had no need to think of any defence that might save my life. The competent Mr Hawkins and the good-looking Mr Tam Pearse would do all that for me and so they did. I followed everything at my trial while I was pretending to follow nothing. It was better that way. Nobody ever asked me to give a written account of what had happened that night, and it certainly was not for me to suggest it. All the others just seemed to accept the state I was pretending to be in. The only one who ever asked me to write anything was the nice woman doctor, Mary Hambly, and even then I kept my replies to a minimum. I had to be very strong with her because she seemed to know that I could follow everything that she was saying. I managed it somehow; I knew I had to, even though she was acting in my defence, she had to be deceived like everyone else. All my hopes were now centred on Trevor. If I had been in two minds about things before the shooting, I was in one mind now. If ever a girl needed a friend and a lover, I did now. I had not been able to tell Trevor this before because the house was full of police and I couldn't say a word, or even exchange a look. After the day of the shooting I saw him only when there were others present; others who did little else but stare at me, and who would certainly have seen if I had made him any sign.

So it remained until the trial itself at the Old Bailey. During the trial, I did manage just once to catch his eye, when we passed in the corridor below the dock when I was on my way back to my cell and he just happened to be there. Or perhaps it was no accident. Just for a moment when the warder's attention was on other things and I took the chance. Once was enough. Our eyes met. I managed to give him a quick wink and he managed a return glance with a smile and a wink. That once was enough. My hopes were buoyed up and I had to try very hard to look bleak, rather than express the joy that I felt once I was back out of the public gaze. So he still cared, in spite of what I had done. If he really had been serious in giving me the information about the law then it seemed that he was right. I listened to all the argument in court and it was clear from the start that Tam Pearse was putting forward a defence based upon hysterical aphonia. I was not surprised since I had read all about this in my own copies of the medical reports which the legal system had been obliged to serve upon me as well as upon my legal advisors.

I listened to the theory that the fatal shot had been fired only by accident, and in the course of our struggle for the gun. I hadn't really thought about that as a possibility before, but I did when Tam Pearse was opening his case, that was my case, to the jury. It was quite true – or it could have been, but then there had been that last shot just as I blacked out and lost all interest in events going on round about me, or had there really been a last shot? I had known nothing for what must have been a good few minutes. Time enough for the police to arrive in large numbers and to get well under way with their enquiries of my startled neighbours and I couldn't really be sure. Everything was more than a little bit hazy. Everything must have been just a little bit hazy for the jury as well, because the judge had told them that if at the end of the day, they were left in any real doubt that the prosecution had made out their case, then I was entitled to the benefit of that doubt; I was entitled to be acquitted and then, of course there came that blissful moment when the jury asked that question which showed that they really were in doubt.

That question meant that I had to be acquitted. It was more difficult than ever to keep up the pose and remain the silent sphinx that I had become, when I heard the judge say that if the jury was in doubt then I had to be acquitted. Not to smile at least. Not to laugh. Not to thank Tam Pearse for everything he had done and for saving my life but I knew I had to keep up the pretence. It was only when Trevor had escorted me and Dr Hambly, and Elsie Collins back to my own home that I began to relax. I heard Elsie ask Dr Hambly what was likely to happen to me now and I heard her reply:

"Well every case differs. Once the cause of the problem has been finally and completely removed, recovery can be very quick, or it can still take months even years, for the patient to get back the powers of speech. We shall just have to wait and see, but it could even be tomorrow. In the cases of shell shock that I dealt with in the past, it was usually only when the soldier was out of all danger, as your friend Isabel is now..."

Then mercifully they made to go and Elsie promised to return with some supper for me. Trevor said that he would get the welfare officer to call round the next day to be sure that I was alright for money. Trevor left the last and gave me a broad wink as he did so. I knew very well that this meant that he would be round again as soon as he could, so I called after Elsie not to bother with the supper since really I felt like nothing more than getting to bed. Then it struck us all at the same moment. I had called after Elsie. Without giving it a thought. I had relaxed after all the weeks of silence, I did not have to fake any more. Just as Dr Hambly had said. Once all the strain was over my powers of speech had come back again. I could not have done it better if it had all still been part of the act. But it wasn't. For the first time I had forgotten that I had been struck dumb just at the moment when I did not have to pretend any more. Then they were congratulating me and life started all over again. I told Elsie that I was going to go straight to bed. Trevor made a point of leaving first, but it was no surprise when my back door opened surreptitiously an hour later and sure enough it was Trevor and it was all as it had been before...

It was providential when the house of a cousin came on the market in Richmond at a good price and Trevor and I found Henry's hidden hoard of money. It proved to be more than enough to finance the purchase of 3, Riverside Terrace, an old Georgian house, once used as part of the mews of the Old Richmond Palace, close to Old Palace Yard. And I was entitled to it. After all I had been his wife and I had a good claim in law to everything that he died possessed of. Trevor had asked a solicitor friend who had explained that when there is no will it is called an intestacy and, in default of any children, or other relations, everything goes to the widow. It was all quite legal. Well, apart from where the money had come from. It was certainly not for me to raise awkward questions about that. Anyway I did not really know where it had come from; didn't they say you should speak no ill of the dead? Everything was going my way at last.

Trevor and I had a quiet marriage but it was marriage, nothing else. Marriage was what I had always believed was the only true way to happiness; although so far perhaps, I hadn't been a very good example of it. I had been very well brought up, and had led a perfectly honest life myself until that moment of madness with the gun.

Life in Richmond was very happy and respectable. I was Mrs Trevor Williams, the lawful wife of a man working in a very respectable solicitors' office. I made new friends. I acquired new interests which included skating at the local ice skating rink in Richmond. I was meeting other young women; I was sublimating a desire to have the children I had been told I never could. But at least I could do baby-sitting for others. I even got invited to the office parties at Ward, Davey and Lewis, the solicitors' firm on Richmond Green where Trevor now worked. Then, just before an office party last Christmas, Trevor told me that he didn't want to go at the last minute. I'd bought a new dress and could not understand why we should fail to turn up when we had already accepted and for what seemed a piffling reason, which he told me was that he had had a row with one of the partners. So I said he should let me know who it was and I would try to be very charming to him and chat up his wife. Reluctantly he agreed to do this and to go to the party as planned but when it came to it, he said that he had already made things up with the partner, so that there was no need for me to. There were lots of people there and I met some nice new ones. After a bit Trevor himself wandered off and I thought nothing of that. I did notice that he was chatting a lot to a very pretty young woman who was much younger than he was and who seemed to be very interested in him but who surely could not really be; so I really should not mind.

I looked again and there they were apparently engrossed in each other; so I did mind. I asked someone who she was and discovered that she was a new articled clerk called Katy. Soon after this Ward, Davey and Lewis started to keep Trevor late at the office, working on a particularly important case that had come up in the High Court in London, he explained. Surely courts always finish at 4.30pm I asked? Oh yes but there was a lot of work to be done after court had finished for the day he explained, and because the case was so important for the firm, it followed it had to be important for him too. He could not refuse. Quite why I did, I don't know but I asked: "...and is Katy engaged on this case too?" And I had my answer. He blushed and agreed she was. Well after that I started looking for all the signs I had seen in my last days with Henry. Trevor started to go to the bathroom every time he was late home and before speaking to me. Just as Henry had done. So I started looking at the towel next day. And sure enough I once found a decided trace of lipstick on it, and it was not my lipstick. I said nothing to Trevor. Surely it could not happen to me all over again? I decided to have a good look round the house. To see the unusual places.

I did not really know why, but in the course of this I had a good look in the garden shed. Trevor was no gardener but an efficient handyman and like many do it yourself experts, he was very proud of his tools, which he guarded jealously and kept in a locked tool box stored in the back of the shed. Just for once I tried to open it and found to my surprise that, Trevor had left it open. So I sifted through the tools. And right down at the bottom, well covered up and wrapped in a duster, there it was. A Colt .45 revolver. Just like the one I had used to shoot Henry six years before. So, very carefully I took it out and examined it. Just as well that I was careful, because I saw at once that it was fully loaded. Then I broke it open, as Trevor had once shown me how to do. There were the six cartridges. But I noticed that one of them had a dent in the middle. It stood out from the others and I knew what it showed. One shot had been fired. What on earth did it all mean? I went back to the day it had all happened at 12,

Clacton Street. I had put it quite out of my mind as part of my past I had no wish to remember. An occasion which had never happened; or if it had then it must have happened to someone else perhaps to a different Isabel, in a different existence, in another place. Of course soon after the event itself, I had gone over it many times, before and during my trial at the Old Bailey. When I had had no friend to talk to. When I could not speak or it might cost me my life. Even then just afterwards I had never been at all clear as to what had happened in the last few moments before I blacked out, as I was just lapsing into unconsciousness. I remembered the great pain in my leg and thinking that Henry must now have the gun himself, and must have pulled the trigger. Unless perhaps it had gone off accidentally. Then he had been standing at the front door at the very moment when I was just losing my senses... did I imagine it or was there then the sound of yet another shot? From the direction of the kitchen? The doctors at the trial had been very clear that the bullet in the brain which had killed Henry, would have done so almost at once. Within a few seconds of the wound being received they had said. Surely there could have been no other Colt .45 involved? The police would have searched the house from top to bottom and they had found no one else was there and no other weapon of any kind.

Then I remembered that at the trial the evidence had been that the first policeman to arrive on the scene had been none other than Trevor. What a coincidence. Or could he have been looking in on passing? None of it made much sense. Then there was the undoubted fact. The fact that a Colt .45, with one shot fired was in Trevor's toolbox six years later. It seemed to me that Trevor had some explaining to do when he got home and he was due quite soon. Just for once he had not told me that he would be likely to be working late. So I put the Colt .45 in the pocket of my apron. I meant to confront Trevor and get the truth out of him. The truth at last. I hurried back into the house and had just got inside when I heard the front door open and there he was. The man I had had a passionate affair with. The man I shared all my secrets with, the man who I was now making my life with, in a second attempt to find true happiness. He was the same good-looking young man I had insisted on marrying. The man I had come to love instead of Henry. Tall dark and handsome; but now he looked nervous and flustered and instead of giving me a kiss and his usual greeting he said:

"Sit down Isabel. I'll get us a drink because I've got something to tell you."

I sat down without a word and waited while he poured out two glasses of white wine and sat down at the table opposite me. He said defiantly:

"I'm afraid that I've fallen in love. For real this time…"

"I thought that you were really in love with me…?"

"Yes, I thought so too."

"It's that Katy Burnley girl at the office? That girl who's young enough to be your daughter almost; if only you had one?"

"She's not as young as all that – and anyway what does age matter? I love her even more than once I thought I loved you."

"Only thought that you loved me? That wasn't what you said at all. You had never loved anyone before me you said – and never would again. Well that's a laugh now. Nothing mattered to you, except for me you used to say; and I've had all the horror of being tried for my life because of you; and I could have been hanged; but nobody would have pointed a finger at the good, up-and-coming Detective Constable Hughes. It was all your idea that I should shoot Henry. Don't deny it. You showed me how to use that Colt revolver. I wouldn't have had a clue how to do it unless you had showed me. You told me all about the woman who had got off a murder rap because she could not speak, so that I'd know how to do it myself. I'd never have done it except for you. And I could have been hanged, when probably it should have been you. That is the point I am beginning to see – it should it have been you all the time?"

"What on earth do you mean?" Trevor looked decidedly uncomfortable as I took the Colt .45 out of my apron pocket and pointed it straight at him.

"And what does this mean? You know where I found it of course, because it is where you kept it hidden. Did you come back to 12, Clacton Street that night, on your way home? Because I thought that somebody else came in just as I blacked out; but then I thought I must have dreamt it. Dreamt that I heard just one more shot as Henry was in the open doorway. But I thought that that was all it was, just a dream. So I never told anyone. Of course I could not speak anyway, since I was following your own scheme of things to escape death by hanging."

"Yes, you kept that up very well indeed. I give you great credit and you kept us both out of trouble. Because I could have been charged with being an accessory, if it had all come out; well we've had a very happy six years in Richmond, haven't we?… but now I've met someone else…"

"So where did this gun come from and what does it all mean? I'm right aren't I? That there was another shot? One shot has been fired from this gun, and only one? And it was in your toolbox which you normally keep locked. Bad luck for you, you forgot just once, but very careless for a policeman who is also a murderer and very careless indeed for a policeman who let someone else take the rap, someone who thought he loved her?"

"I did love you. It was the only way. I always thought you'd be a rotten shot but it was really coincidence that I happened to find that gun at the station. It was just coincidence that I had it in my pocket when I was passing by on my way home that night and heard the shooting break out…"

"And it was just coincidence that you let me be tried for murder when all the time it should have been you?"

I could hear my voice rising. We had never really discussed that night in March 1961 before. We had been too happy and I at least, had not wanted to risk ruining it all by going over the past, when the present was so good. I still had the gun in my hand but the safety catch was on. I remembered very clearly what Trevor himself had taught me and now I pushed it from "safe" to "fire". Trevor saw me do it and went completely white.

"Please put that gun down."

"All the time it should have been you, and now you want to run off and leave me, you bastard. Just like Henry and Irene Barret and you really think that I'd let you get away with that?"

"Please be reasonable. You couldn't tell the police all this. They'd never believe you. After all that evidence at your trial they could never admit they'd been wrong all the time; but please put that gun down now, you are very dangerous."

And he came round the table and started to move towards me. So I shot him. I didn't think; I just did it. Just once, without a further thought. He had done just what Henry had done six years ago. It was too much. So I shot him in the head and he fell down at my feet and I knew that he was dead. This time it had needed only one shot, but of course he was facing me and was very close. Or perhaps my aim had improved with practice, I thought cynically. To have it happen all over again had sent me berserk. To have the man I loved calmly say that he was not in love with me at all, that he was leaving me for a younger woman, on top of discovering that if the truth had been known I should never have been charged with murdering Henry at all, was too much. What you have done once it is all too easy to do again. It was not so much revenge this time, as the administration of justice and this time I did not pass out.

I knew very well that the law had changed. That the halfway house, when some murderers were still punished by hanging while others were not, had gone. The distinction between capital and non capital murder had always been illogical and now death by hanging for murder was a thing of the past. For any murder. Trevor himself had explained it to me;

235

now here I was with a dead man and once more, we had been the only people in the house. Then there came a ringing of the bell. So a neighbour must have heard the sound of the shot and what was I to do? Perhaps I would not hang but the thought of a life sentence of imprisonment was appalling. My experiences on the last occasion had certainly taught me that. I hated being shut up. The rotten food they gave you in prison. On top of that I had loathed being bossed about by wardresses. I had hated it all; so what was I to do? What had worked once might work again? It was the only thing I could think of. Perhaps it would – after all why not? Anyway it was the only thing that I could try. So I had to try it and be just as good at acting like a silent moron as I had been before.

Then there was banging at the door and the bell was rung again and it was held down. Almost by instinct I went to open it; but then I remembered just in time that I must be shell-shocked again. So I waited while the knocking got louder and I could hear the sound of voices discussing what to do and I recognised the voice of George Clark my immediate neighbour and I heard the words "get the police". So I let them call the police and I stayed silent while they forced open my front door; and I stayed silent when the police came, and then the doctor and then the ambulance men, to take away Trevor's body. It was all like a ghastly recurring nightmare; and it all went on just the same as it had those six years before. There was the sympathetic, or at least apparently sympathetic, policewoman; and then I was taken to the police station and examined by the doctors; and I stayed silent all the time. I knew how to do it after all and it seemed to be working just as well for the second time as it had for the first because I heard one of the doctors mention the phrase "hysterical aphonia" and I thought that perhaps I had won. At least perhaps I might not be convicted of murder.

I also heard that they were trying to track down the Colt .45 and I thought that that was all to the good, because I thought that they would never be able to and that at least they would probably realise that it was not likely to have belonged to me. With my scanty knowledge of the workings of the legal mind, I wondered how could a court of law rule out the possibility that Trevor had committed suicide? After all there was nobody there but him and me, and he was dead, and I was not saying a word. So how could anybody be sure about what had happened? I remembered very well how my own judge, in my own case, had emphasised to the jury in his summing up of my case, that they could not possibly convict me of anything unless they were absolutely sure that I was guilty; so there was hope at least, and as the days passed my hopes grew. It was a pity that I could not go to Tam Pearse or to Mr Hawkins to represent me but that would obviously be impossible. However that very good Richmond firm of solicitors, Pettigrews had been allocated to me. I had been offered representation by Ward, Davey and Lewis, but I had turned it down. They could not have known about Trevor and Katy Burnley of course, but if they could not see that there might be a conflict of interest, then I certainly could. Mr Simpson of Pettigrews, was quite optimistic.

Thank heavens they had not sent me to Broadmoor this time, but only to a Remand Hostel where my solicitor could come and see me. He told me what he thought about it all while I listened in silence. This time the doctors called by the prosecution had come to the same conclusion as only Dr Hambly had before and Mr Simpson thought that there was a very good

237

chance that I might not be sent for trial at all because of insufficient evidence. Even if I were brought to trial, what I could get away with once I could surely get away with again I thought. I should be so much better able to see the traps. For one thing I found it much easier to stay silent; practice makes perfect after all. I started to write shaky notes on the paper he provided me with, but I was very careful to see that they were themselves almost as confused as I was thought to be.

Then, after three days had passed I was sitting in my cell drinking a cup of quite good tea and relaxing and really beginning to think that I was going to achieve the seemingly impossible by killing two men who had, at least once, loved me and escaping just retribution, when there was a crash at the door, and it burst open and in walked the still familiar figure of Detective Chief Inspector Hollingsworth.

"Hello, Mrs Earle or is it Mrs Hughes, or is it Mrs Williams this time? They say you have been struck dumb again?... how very convenient!... but lightening never strikes twice does it?"

So there it was. I was really caught out, they must have been able to trace that wretched Colt .45 after all, and I said, yes in the shock of seeing Hollingsworth I quite forgot and I really blew everything because I said:

"Oh God! It would have to be you of all people..." and I looked up to see the smile of triumph on his face.

Postscript

"What is truth?" said jesting Pilate.

Isabel was a real person. Henry was her husband and he was a Minder and died as described. Everything about her and her trial is the truth as far as I can remember it. Except for the result. She was not called Isabel Earle and her personal details have been changed to prevent disclosing her identity, because the real Isabel is still alive. But her case is a tiny part of legal history and figures in the Law Reports. What really happened is all set out (except for the result) in chapters one and two, from the point of view of the author, who was the barrister who defended her at the Old Bailey. The judge who tried the case did have his duty to protect the public well in mind. He made it quite clear in his summing up to the jury that he at least, did not believe for a moment that it could all have been an accident. There had been two well-qualified psychiatrists who gave evidence for the Crown that the lady was insane. And if she was insane, he clearly (and rightly) thought that she should go to Broadmoor, so as to receive treatment if any was found possible, but also because she would then cease to be a danger to the public.

What was not quite so clearly right was that he made his personal views very clear to the jury. A judge is meant to direct the jury as to the law but to leave all decisions of fact for them to decide and not to make his own views so obvious as to influence them. Had this judge leant much too far in favour of the prosecution by making it too obvious that he believed that they were right on the two main issues? Firstly on the issue of guilt of murder, so that the jury could safely reject the possibility that the fatal shot might have been fired accidentally, and secondly by rejecting the possibility that Isabel was only "shell-shocked", and so not insane at all which would have meant a finding of diminished responsibility, so not murder but only manslaughter and some much lesser penalty.

At the time I certainly thought that he had gone over the line and usurped the function of the jury, for the best of motives no doubt. So I advised my solicitors to appeal the decision to the Court of Criminal Appeal. And they did. And the appeal failed. For a reason quite as absurd as the illogical classifications which divided capital murder from non-capital murder under the provisions of the Homicide Act 1957, and that was that it was only possible for the defence to appeal against a conviction – and a verdict of "guilty but insane" was not a conviction but an acquittal. The case of Rex versus Felstead, decided in 1914 said so, and it has never been repealed, and any decision of the House of Lords is binding on every other court and can only be overturned by a further decision of the House of Lords itself, so that regrettably this injustice remains a part of our law today. It should certainly be changed. The case of Felstead was decided in the House of Lords and my application for leave to appeal to that most superior court was refused. Could it even be possible that as a result of writing this book it might be changed now? Because it is clearly unjust, that if a defendant has committed no crime, he could still be wrongly convicted and sent to Broadmoor perhaps for the rest of his life, with no right of appeal at all. So 'bad luck Isabel Earle, in Broadmoor you will stay' was the result of her appeal which came on for hearing in 1961 before the Lord Chief Justice, Lord Parker and two other judges of the High Court and is reported in the Law Reports. Part of it reads:

"A verdict was returned by the jury at the trial in these terms 'guilty of manslaughter but insane. Not guilty of capital murder', and on the direction of the learned judge the record was made up as reading 'guilty of the act charged but insane'. The appellant now appeals to this court against what she terms her conviction and her sentence. Mr Wheatley who appears on her behalf, quite rightly abandons any question of appeal against sentence because, if the verdict stands, the sentence, which was that she was to be kept in custody until Her Majesty's pleasure, be known, is statutory and there could be no other alternative. Notwithstanding that verdict and record, Mr Wheatley maintains that he is entitled to appeal to this court and to show, if he can, that the learned judge misdirected the jury on the question of whether the act charged had been committed. Quite shortly it is said that the learned judge misdirected the jury, that in the case of a sane person the verdict must on the evidence be one of murder or manslaughter, and that there was no room for an acquittal. It is said that the learned judge was wrong in so directing the jury and that the appellant is entitled to appeal to this court.

The difficulty with which Mr Wheatley is at once faced is that by the Criminal Appeal Act 1907, an appeal is only given to a person convicted on indictment. The question is whether this verdict represents a conviction on indictment. The matter was put beyond doubt some 47 years ago in Felstead's case in which the House of Lords held that this verdict is an acquittal, and accordingly the Court of Criminal Appeal has no jurisdiction in the matter... accordingly this appeal is dismissed..." I knew all about the case of Felstead and believed it did not apply to Isabel's case at all because the facts were different and in Felstead's case the only issue was whether or not Felstead was insane, not whether or not he was guilty at all. And no-body is guilty of any crime if the death is the result of an accident, as I tried to persuade the jury that this had been.

When I thought I would write about it I knew that I had to find out the truth if I could. Surely it would be easy after all these years? Had Dr Hambly been right in saying that Isabel suffered from hysterical aphonia? Or had the other doctors been right that she was insane? Or had neither of them been right and had Isabel been a shrewd and accomplished actress? So I wrote to the Medical Superintendant of Broadmoor, explaining my interest and asking what had happened to the real Isabel Earle. But patient confidentiality came into the matter and he could not tell me. So I asked if I could write to the lady but was told that she was no longer a patient. So she was still alive? Reluctantly he agreed that she was. So when had she been discharged? He could not tell me – patient confidentiality again. So I was stuck and could only write about the fictional figure, Isabel Earle. Apart from the first two chapters it is fiction. The real Isabel is still alive. She was sent to Broadmoor who at least were able to tell me that she had been released but when? They will not say.

Could she have been faking it all the time? Well that of course is straying into the realms of fiction – and I do hope you enjoyed reading it!